Other Related Books by Charles Meadow

Text Information Retrieval Systems, (with others) 2007
Messages, Meaning and Symbols, 2006
Making Connections: Communications Through the Years, 2002
Ink into Bits: A Web of Converging Media, 1998
Telecommunications for Management (with A.S. Tedesco),1985
Sounds and Signals: How We Communicate (Juvenile), 1975
Man-Machine Communication, 1970

The Number One One Dog in Victoria

Charles T. Meadow

Order this book online at www.trafford.com
or email orders@trafford.com

Most Trafford titles are also available at major online book retailers.

Note for Librarians: A cataloguing record for this book is available from Library
and Archives Canada at www.collectionscanada.ca/amicus/index-e.html

Printed in Victoria, BC, Canada.

ISBN: 978-1-4251-7500-9 (soft)
ISBN: 978-1-4251-7501-6 (ebook)

*Our mission is to efficiently provide the world's finest, most comprehensive book publishing
service, enabling every author to experience success. To find out how to publish your book, your
way, and have it available worldwide, visit us online at www.trafford.com*

Trafford rev. 10/19/2009

www.trafford.com

North America & international
toll-free: 1 888 232 4444 (USA & Canada)
phone: 250 383 6864 ◆ fax: 812 355 4082

This book is dedicated to my immediate family, human and canine, all of whom contributed to my understanding of relationships, human and canine:

Mary Louise
Debra and Paul
   Leah
   Sam
   Tucker
Sandra and Victor
   Eli
   Satchel
Alison and Dan
   Hailie
Ben
Crispin

Acknowledgments

It may sound trite but is nonetheless true. Books are rarely done entirely by a single person. My thanks to the following, listed in alphabetic order, who read and suggested needed changes in the manuscript at various stages, gave ideas on illustration, or who contributed illustrations:

Prof. Geraldine Allen
Kirsten Bishopric
Jean Chen
Prof. Leland Donald
Prof. Bonnie Frick
Dr. Stephen Frick
Dr. Mary Anne Leason
Marilyn Mahan
Ben Meadow
Debra Meadow
Mary Louise Meadow
Sandra Meadow
A.R. Ratsoy
Beth Stevenson
Karen Whyte.

About the Author

Charles Meadow is Professor Emeritus, Faculty of Information, University of Toronto. He has published a dozen books, mainly on computers and communications and has edited two professional journals. Recent books of interest are *Making Connections: Communications Through the Ages* and *Messages, Meaning, and Symbols: The Communication of Information*. His research interest evolved from developing information retrieval systems to communication between users and these systems, and this led to interest in communication in general and then to communication with dogs. In addition to this professional interest, he has had a life-long interest in dogs and cats. He has established a special relationship with Crispin, the subject of this book, and vice versa. Meadow, a dual citizen of Canada and the United States, formerly taught at Drexel University in Philadelphia, worked for, among others, General Electric, IBM, and the U.S. federal government, and served in the U.S. Marines. He now lives with his wife, Mary Louise, in Victoria, British Columbia. Four grown children are scattered along the edges of the Pacific Ocean. Crispin, wholly Canadian, frequently visits canine cousins in the U.S.

Contents

PART IV   Recognition

PART I   In the Beginning. . .

We decide to get a dog and his life with us as a growing puppy.

1 About This Book

THIS BOOK is about a dog and myself, his owner, keeper, leader of his pack or, as known among other dog owners, father of the dog. It is also about dogs in general. It is the story of my dog and our lives together and a little about animal science. Since he came to us as a puppy, he learned much from me, but I also learned much from him. Some I learned on my own initiative; some because he motivated me to read a lot about dogs and other animals. From this I learned a great deal but mainly I came to a deeper appreciation of animals and our joint roles in nature. I am fascinated at the way members of different species have come together as one family and have learned about each other's ways of communicating and ways of living.

Our life together has had its ups and downs. Mostly, he is a delight to have around. From when he first came to live with us, and continuing to this day, we are often stopped in the street for compli-

Figure 1. The author and his dog. Photo by Mary Louise Meadow.

ments on his good looks and sterling behaviour. On the other side of the coin, we once had the police call on us and, even worse, a lawyer. Here is our story, warts and all.

What brought me to write this? I have written all or part of a dozen books, about computers, databases, and communications. This is a different kind of book. It is a highly personal view of my dog and myself, how I feel about him, how I react to him, how he has affected me. I was fascinated to learn that dogs really do have personalities and that they can understand us, our feelings, and our likely reaction to certain tricks they might play on us.

What does the book's title mean? All is revealed in chapter 20.

When my wife, Mary Louise, and I first began to consider getting a dog, I thought in terms of getting a pet, something animate to play and go for walks with. I soon learned that a dog is not a toy, but a true member of the family, although of a different species. The idea of a member of another species being a member of our family was new to me, even though I have had dogs before. But this is what happened. We have our differences and similarities; the more of both we understand, the closer the relationship grows.

When I set out to write this book, I thought I would phrase it from his point of view, make it seem he was writing it. I quickly found that to be impossible because some of what I wanted to say is clearly beyond a dog's ability to understand and certainly to express at an adult human level. Instead, I insert comments that I imagine he would say about what I had just written, if he could write or even think in our words. Of course, it can't really be in his words – he doesn't have any. His comments are what I imagine, or perhaps just hope, he might say. They are set off

in a different type face and signed, this way.

I might as well start out modestly admitting that the hero of this story is the best looking and nicest dog I know. But I am aware I am not unique in these feelings, not the only pet owner who is fascinated at species-to-species communication or of having a dog companion. I don't get tired of this; my fascination grows each year as I come to understand him more and more. I hope our story will interest other owners and assure them their problems are not unique and their attachment is understood. Although I have had other pets, I never anticipated the way this dog would affect my life. He is simply a joy to have around.

A philosopher once wrote that, "If a lion could talk, we would not understand him."[1] In other words, our instincts, our culture, our values, our physical make up, our senses of perception, and ways of making associations and drawing conclusions are so different probably neither party could know what the other was saying, even with a mutually understood vocabulary and grammar.

A dog's sense of smell is so superior to ours that if he could tell us what he understands from a few sniffs, we might not believe that so much information can come from a quick sniff of another dog's behind. Some birds can sense a magnetic field and use this for navi-

Figure 2. Humans and lions cannot converse with each other as humans can with each other, but limited verbal communication is possible between people and animals. Drawing by A.R. Ratsoy.

gating on those long migration trips.[2] What do they really sense? What tells them they are off-course? Even if they knew English, could they explain this form of navigation? I often talk to my dog on walks but I don't sense that he understands a single word I say, other than "sit," "stay" or "go" or the like.

The book starts with some history of the dog and me, moves on to reminiscences of him as he grew from puppy to adult, and then some discussion of dogs' history in general, means of communication, intelligence, and emotions. These final chapters are more about evolution and behavioural science than about an individual dog. The discussion of a puppy's bathroom habits does not sound of great importance to the study of communication or understanding, but it is. As I'll discuss later, he is a *feng shui* advocate. Location and sometimes even orientation are of great importance to him when it is time to go.

There are debates about whether dogs can think, whether they use language, whether they can laugh or feel love. Some scientists in the field tend to believe animals do none of these. I have noticed in my reading different beliefs by serious scientists on the one hand and people who live with animals in a close relationship on the other hand. (There are those who are both, and more scientists are beginning to recognize that thinking and emotions do occur in dogs and other animals.) When we take the animals into our homes and treat them as members of our family we may see one set of behavioural characteristics. When the dogs are merely subjects to be observed or tested while doing tasks not normal to the lives of animals in the wild, we might see different behaviour.

For now, let us leave it that dogs can learn to obey commands, do not appear to understand the concept of future and, while they do have some remembrance of things past, they have not the same ability to recall as humans do. Do they think? This is a question that may be easy to answer once the poser of the question comes up with a clear definition of what the word *think* means. Warning: that last is not easy. Do they have a language? The answer is pretty much the same.

None of the limits scientists tend to ascribe to animal cognition mean that dogs are not thoroughly lovable creatures or that they do not give their form of love as well as receive our form.

Finally, my academic background requires of me that I provide source information for ideas taken from others or to recommend further reading. To do this I put all references in the Notes section at the end and insert a note number in the text this way[n]. It may refer to a single quotation or a list of relevant sources and include some comments by me, as well as recommended readings. A Bibliography follows the Notes, with complete bibliographic citations.

What's a book?

2 Pondering Previous Pets

BEFORE INVITING a dog into our family, there had to be a decision to find the right one. I have always liked animals but I grew up in cities and in a household that was usually busy, with no one to devote serious time to caring for a dog. We once had one when I was about seven. I liked having him, as did my brother, but like many children today we were more inclined to play with him occasionally than do the chores of walking him two or three times a day or bathing him. In those days, dogs ran free on the streets and there were no poop-and-scoop laws even if his deposit was made in the street or on someone's lawn. If I had been asked to do that cleaning up, I would have been horror stricken, but I see kids today who do the job routinely.

As I reflected on why I liked animals when I was young, I think that part of the attraction may have been the typical one of wishing there were someone around who was lower than me (youngest child) in the family hierarchy. As an adult, there is more to it. I have often felt in awe of large mountains. I am continually fascinated by the sea. The psychiatrist Carl Jung once visited New Mexico and reported a conversation with a local native man who said to him, "Do you not think that all life comes from the mountain?"[1] I've heard similar sentiments about other aspects of nature. Certainly, in a sense, the sea is literally the mother of us all, if we accept that animal life originated there. When I see animals in the wild, including even the crows who raise hell outside our window in the early morning, I feel in touch with nature. I think that even a domestic animal, cat, dog, horse, or whatever, can give some of the same feeling. They are part of what we are part of; we're all related.

Chief Seattle, of the Puget Sound Suquamish Tribe, and the man for whom the city was named, was said to have put it this way:

> [T]he white man must treat the beasts of this land as his brothers.... What is man without the beasts? If all the beasts were gone, man would die from a great loneliness of spirit. For whatever happens to the beasts, also happens to the man. All things are connected.[2]

Figure 3. Chief Seattle. There are several images of him that do not look much alike. This is a statue sculpted by James Wehn, placed in Tilikum Square, Seattle in his honor. Photo by Ben Meadow.

When I became a parent myself our family had the usual array of pets: cats, gerbils, goldfish, and a rabbit, few of whom stayed for long. One of our cats, Max, was with us for 15 years and he was a great family favorite. The other cats simply disappeared. At one time, we had a cottage in an enclave within a large, forested, provincial park. There, the rabbit had a roomy outdoor pen from which he escaped. He looked so beautiful while running free that we let him go into the woods and wished him luck. There were no predators in the park as far as we knew.

Figure 4. Max, our beloved and loyal cat, who followed us on our many moves and adapted quickly each time Photo by one of the Meadows. (We forgot which.)

Our first family dog when I was an adult was procured because we needed a watchdog due to a string of burglaries. Sam, as he was called, was an adult, a mongrel of un-known descent. He came from a friend of friends and had lived all his adult life in an apartment, which should have suggested that maybe he didn't meet too many people of all types and ages. He was a great watchdog but could not tolerate small children. He was nerv-ous at their quick movements and snapped at more than one of them. We had two children under the age of four at the time. It was Sam who had to go.

Sam's replacement, a Brittany Spaniel named Shane, was a beauti-ful dog with a pleasant disposition. We found him in the local animal shelter. His problem seemed to be his webbed paws, common among the so-called water dogs that go into water to retrieve a victim. The webbing, of course, constituted built-in swim fins. I would not have believed it if I had not seen how quickly those huge paws could dig a tunnel under our fence and set him free. Then he would wander the neighbourhood, a practice not permitted in our town. Because he was so handsome and nice he would be caught and brought to our vet, whose tag he wore. I would be summoned both to take him home and reward the finder, a few too many times. With regret, we returned him to the shelter from whence he came and, with that, we gave up on dogs for a while.

The while wasn't very long. A friend saw an ad in the paper for a placid dog rescued after he appeared to have been hit by a car. The rescuers took care of him, got a veterinarian to see to his injuries, but found one of their children to be allergic to him. He was a fine looking Yellow Labrador Retriever, probably with some German Shepherd mixed in. He also had some remaining illnesses which led to large vet bills for us. But, he was a truly nice, very gentle dog. He attached himself to me but did not demand a monopoly on access as some dogs do. He would sit or lie next to where I was then get up and follow me wherever I went around the house. So we named him Shadow.

What could possibly go wrong with such a fine fellow? He could climb and jump. He could and did climb fences, something I had never before seen a dog do. If a fence was no more than four feet high,

Figure 5. Sam, my first dog as an adult. A great watchdog but bad with children. As a result, he had to go. Photo by C. Meadow.

Figure 6. A facsimile of Shane, of whom we could find no pictures. He looked like this fellow, but had more brown, less white in his coat. Photo courtesy Ataboy Brittanys Shelly Grant.

he could jump over it, looking so graceful as he did that it was impossible to be mad at him. He, too, would escape and wander around, but he tended to go into stores and make himself at home. He never did any harm, but shop owners were not thrilled. At this time I knew some people who had a hobby farm in the suburbs and we thought he might do well if sent to live there, so he and we were invited for a try-out. While we were being shown around the property, Shadow was put into a pen that was about ten square meters, with a three-meter high fence around it. Before long, four of us watched, astonished, as Shadow climbed up and over, jumped down, went to the road, and began chasing cars.

Guess who was not invited back.

We gave up. We could not control him, and thus ended our dog owning for quite a few years. During that time we had some overseas travel and some friends in another city took care of Max, so we didn't miss having a pet when we returned.

Later, as I became far more knowledgeable about dogs, I began to wonder why these things happened. Why did we give up on three dogs in rapid succession? The first decision was easy. Sam was quite neurotic. He

Figure 7. This should be Shadow but we cannot find any pictures of him either. He looked much like this white German Shepherd. We believed Shadow was a mix of a dog such as this with a Yellow Labrador Retriever. This is a friendly, happy looking dog, as was Shadow, but his ears were smaller. Photo © iStockphoto.com/ LUGO.

could not tolerate active kids and we had a baby still in the crawling stage. It rather quickly became apparent that we had no choice. Out he went although he had proven himself an effective and courageous watch dog.

Shane and Shadow were caught in a situation I have since heard about. Owners get a dog without realizing what they are getting into. Both these dogs had lovely dispositions but were capable of escaping our rather large, fenced yard and the dogs needed more human attention than we were able to give at the time. We had jobs and small children to take care of as well as a yard that was designed by a Hollywood horror film set designer. There weren't any crazed murderers or prehistoric animals, but the green stuff, in some places, never stopped growing and in others never appeared. It sometimes seemed the yard took more care than the children or the dog.

Clearly, we were not ready for a dog. Shane had come from the shelter. In retrospect it seemed he may have been sent there because of the same problem we had. Anyway, back he went. If Shadow had not been rescued by our neighbour, he probably would have been picked up by the police or an animal control officer and ended up in the same shelter. These excuses don't acquit us, but at least we can take some consolation from knowing their behaviour wasn't entirely our fault. A more experienced owner or a trainer might have known how to alter that behaviour. Also, we never had the time or understanding of the need for bonding with these dogs, except for Shadow who initiated the bonding. Indeed, they were pets, not family members.

The decision to get a dog, we have since found, means committing time, tolerating idiosyncrasies such as shedding, barking, chewing, or escaping, and learning how to welcome a dog into the family pack.

Some twenty-five years after Shadow's departure, I retired but still went to my office frequently, taught some classes, and did much writing. Much of this was done at home and it became common for Mary Louise, to come home in the afternoon and say something like, "It's a glorious day. Have you been out?" I'd look at my watch, realize the entire day had gone by, and mutter, guiltily, "No." To change this, to get me out of the house more, we decided on a puppy.

> This was all before my time in what is now my pack. But I'm glad to hear that my pack leader realizes he and I, and all dogs and people, are related. But, I don't really feel related to cats and other small creatures. When I see them, I just get an urge to kill them. I don't know why.

The comment above was written in early 2008. Near the end of that year Crispin began to show interest in making friends with cats. It isn't every cat he meets, but there have been distinct signs of progress toward peace.

3 Deciding

WE BEGAN to look at dogs in the neighbourhood. Some we saw out walking and some in the near-by animal shelter. Because we lived in an apartment, we felt a small dog would be best although I preferred a dog who barked, if noise were needed, rather than yapped as very small dogs seem to do. In other words, a bass or tenor, not a soprano. We later learned from people who had large dogs in even smaller apartments that their dogs sleep all the time at home. So size doesn't seem to matter much, as long as the dogs get out often. We were too ignorant to think of such issues as shedding or the personality of the various breeds. We would have been content with a small mongrel. The shelter had only large dogs. A staff member explained that many people acquire cute little puppies, then become alarmed as they grow into 35-40 kilogram food consumption factories. The few small dogs that come to this shelter come in the morning and are normally gone in a few hours.

Mary Louise met some people walking Wheaten Terriers, a breed I had never heard of. She thought they were good looking dogs, with pleasant dispositions, and about the right size. We began to look for advertisements for such dogs. The closest we found was an ad for a Schwheaten, a Miniature Schnauzer-Wheaten Terrier cross. And so, with a trip to the breeder who had advertised, the real story finally begins.

🐕 🐕 🐕

Our hero was born on June 19, 2000 in the small town of Terra Cotta, Ontario. For his first four months he lived there with his mother and four brothers and sisters. The owner, the breeder, fed them, was a friend to them, let them out to exercise, and took the dogs for rides to the vet, but they remained housed with and under control of their canine mother. The pups and their mother lived in a barn.

Litter mates went away, one at a time, until only two were left. One of these was taken by his new owner while we were examining the last of the litter. We had agreed before making our foray that, since this was the first dog we would consider buying, we were not going to buy right away, no matter what.

We were to learn that, in dog licensing and insurance circles, a Schwheaten is just called a Mixed Terrier. I also learned later that another name for such a dog is Wheatzer and that the mother of this letter was a Miniature Schnauzer, the father a true Schwheaten – half and half.. The father, I was told, had not been invited to express his affections to the mother, at least not by the breeder-owner of a pure-bred female.

When we arrived at the owner's miniature farm-like setting, the owner took the puppy outside and sat him on a tree stump serving as a table. She said all kinds of nice things about him, but we just looked and petted him. The little fellow was of a shaggy grey colour. The brother, who was taken away while we were there, was all wheat coloured, a yellowish tan. "Our" puppy was so cute I could not entertain the thought of not buying him. Regardless of colour, my mind was immediately made up. I am without sales resistance.

I backed away and watched Mary Louise watching him. I was afraid I might have to do a sales job on her, but she had a grin that could have gone from Terra Cotta to Vancouver. Then, it occurred to me that the little guy looked like Crispin, the dog hero of a children's book I used to read to my children. That dog's full name was Crispin's Crispian, an odd name, but it was an odd story and we loved it. Right then I suggested Crispin for his name and Mary Louise cheerfully agreed. A deal was quickly closed for the purchase. So much for planning and sensible intentions.

It happened that we were planning to go away for the coming weekend so we agreed to pick him up the following Tuesday, which was to be October 24, 2000.

> I didn't know what was going on here. I was sad to see my brother picked up and carried off by a strange person. I never thought such a terrible thing could happen to me.

🐾

Between decision and delivery, as with the coming birth of a first child, there is shopping to be done. The dog, like the child, needs a place to sleep suited to his size and physical needs. For the child there are clothes, including diapers. For the dog there is a leash and collar. For both there is the need for feeding implements suited to the newcomer's expected manner of eating and drinking. For sleeping, all the dog books recommend what they call a crate, actually a wire cage. These are readily available in pet shops and the suggestions are that the best kind is fitted to his size, not the biggest the owners can afford. Dogs feel safe in a snug space. They also need something soft to sleep on. An old bed pillow of ours sufficed and, although since replaced, that type bedding is still in use. We did not continue use of the crate as Crispin grew up.

The books all recommend not one of those extendable leashes for a puppy, but about a two-meter, fixed length one. This gives better control over a puppy inclined to wander, which it turned out Crispin did and does. Settled. Then we got a neck collar, a lucky guess because we found the larger harnesses kept coming off him and smaller ones chafed his legs.

Now, dogs don't need spoons and forks, but they do need dishes which should be fitting for the royal self. So, separate dishes for solid food and drink were carefully thought about and procured, although they were pretty much like the ones everyone else thinks about and gets. Mostly, the differences among them were only size or decoration. The water dish is carefully designed to be virtually impossible to tip over. The food dish is too heavy for a small dog to tip and nearly impossible for him to pick up in his teeth.

🐕 🐕 🐕

Also during the interim, I felt I had heard the name Crispin somewhere recently, but couldn't place it. We looked in an encyclopedia. It is the name of an obscure saint who lived in the third century. He had a brother, also a saint, named either Crispian or Crispinian. They were of Italian origin but lived in France. As a result of this move to different linguistic areas their names are often spelled differently and the unimaginative naming added to the confusion. According to tradition the brothers were patron saints of leather workers, the trade they followed.[1] That more or less explained the odd name of the dog in the story, but not where I had heard it recently.

The encyclopedia article also mentioned Shakespeare and that struck a chord as we had recently seen the Kenneth Branagh film *Henry V*. That is where Henry makes the famous, rousing speech to his army, just before the Battle of Agincourt on October 25, 1415. This date was and still is known as St. Crispin's Day. Henry, or Kenneth, said the often quoted words found at the end of this chapter.

Figure 8. Sir Lawrence Olivier in his portrayal of Heny V, addressing his troops on the eve of the Battle of Agincourt on St. Crispin's Day. It was this address that contained the words quoted on p. 25. This is a still from a 1944 version of *Henry V*, produced by Two Cities Films.

Shakespeare tended to use Crispin or Crispian, or both, inter-changeably. A copy of that speech hung over our Crispin's crate until we moved and he gave up sleeping in just one place, but it's still on the wall in our bedroom which is also his.

On the appointed day for getting Crispin, the breeder called and asked if we would mind picking him up the next day, instead. Mild disappointment but no real problem, so we readily agreed. That put the memorable date on October 25, St. Crispin's Day, a happy coinci-dence for us and, as Mary Louise likes to say, a good example of Jungian synchronicity.

The book I used to read to my eldest child, Debra, got lost some-where. When the real Crispin came into our lives I tried to find a copy. I thought Crispin's Crispian was in its title, but it was not and that made it hard for me to find. Eventually, I remembered the author was the famous Margaret Wise Brown, better known by all North Ameri-can parents for her wonderful book, *Goodnight, Moon*. Then I found the Crispin book's title was *Mr. Dog*.[2] It was a Little Golden Book, not often found in libraries, and it was some years before Debra managed to find a used copy. We treasure it. When I finally got to see it again, it turned out that the fictional Crispin was an Airedale, a Terrier but brown. Our Crispin was the colour of a Schnauzer, grey. The faces were the same except for the colour. The breeder told us that he might yet turn blond, but what actually happened is that his black hairs turned mostly light grey or pewter colour. Occasionally, we see a bit of wheaten colour coming through and then disappearing again. Why, we don't know.

🐕 🐕 🐕

On the day of collecting Crispin, he wasn't thrilled to be packed into a strange car and driven away by a strange person. I stopped at a park on the way home, to let him get out, walk and get used to me.

Figure 9. Crispin's Crispian is on the left and his name-sake Crispin is on the right. They may not look alike here, but Crispin came into my life some 40 years after the book was lost. The colour is, of course, different, Crispin hates to wear a hat, and he doesn't smoke. The book cover shown is from *Mister Dog* by Margaret Wise Brown and illustrated. by Garth Williams, © 1952, renewed 1980 by Random House, Inc. Used by permission of Golden Books, an imprint of Random House Children's Books, a division of Random House, Inc.

He showed no sign of wanting to get used to me – not aggressive, just uninterested, as if he wished he could find a hole to crawl into. He was unaffected by the auspicious date or his exalted new name, but we got home without incident and, as I quickly learned, nothing makes a dog so happy as food.

"Not thrilled . . . crawl into a hole"? What did he expect? I'm packed into a car by a stranger, leaving all I had ever known be-hind, of place, people, smells, other dogs. I had never been in a car for as long as I was that day and when we got to what was to become my new home it seemed very strange. No grass to play in, no other dogs to play with. Outside, there were many, many strange people and many noisy animals that seemed to be called

cars, trucks, street cars, and motorcycles. I hated the motorcycles the most but I could never catch one.

My new pack consisted of a human male and female and me.
They were nice to me, fed me well, and took me for walks. There
was grass near by. But I could only go for a walk with a rope
around my neck. How would you like that? They also followed me
and, if I pooped, picked it up in a little bag. I don't know what
they did with it and I can't figure out why they would do that.

The St. Crispin's Day Speech.

This day is call'd the feast of Crispian.
He that outlives this day, and comes safe home,
Will stand a tip-toe when this day is nam'd,
And rouse him at the name of Crispian.
He that shall live this day, and see old age,
Will yearly on the vigil feast his neighbours,
And say 'To-morrow is Saint Crispian.'
Then will he strip his sleeve and show his scars,
And say 'These wounds I had on Crispian's day.'
Old men forget; yet all shall be forgot,
But he'll remember, with advantages,
What feats he did that day. Then shall our names,
Familiar in his mouth as household words-
Harry the King, Bedford and Exeter,
Warwick and Talbot, Salisbury and Gloucester-
Be in their flowing cups freshly rememb'red.
This story shall the good man teach his son;
And Crispin Crispian shall ne'er go by,
From this day to the ending of the world,
But we in it shall be remembered-
We few, we happy few, we band of brothers;
For he to-day that sheds his blood with me
Shall be my brother; be he ne'er so vile,
This day shall gentle his condition;
And gentlemen in England now-a-bed
Shall think themselves accurs'd they were not here,
And hold their manhoods cheap whiles any speaks
That fought with us upon Saint Crispin's day.

WILLIAM SHAKESPEARE, HENRY V, ACT 4, SCENE 3

4 BONDING

EVEN BEFORE St. Crispin's Day, I had bought a book called *I Just Got a Puppy. What Do I Do?*[1] This book gave some great advice, the most valuable being that the new owner and dog should spend the first week together just bonding. Put off training and any discipline until later. The authors also advised socializing the dog. Take him with you to as many different places and to meet as many different people as possible.

But our first concern, advice or no advice, was for the prospect of "accidents." Well, they are not accidents to the dog. He relieves himself where and when he feels the need, although the choice of place was to change later on. More on this critical subject is in the next chapter.

How does a grown person bond with another person, not previously known, in the space of about a week? For my answer, I had to remember when my first child was due to be born. A friend told me that the birth of a first child would change me more than anything else that had ever happened to me. I suppose I must except my own birth. More of a change, he said, than finishing school, starting a career, or getting married. I had almost no experience of babies. I was the second and younger of two children in my family. I never had any cousins that I knew as babies. I never baby-sat. So, I didn't make much of my friend's remark until THE DAY. Back in the 1950s, fathers did not normally sit with their wives in a labour room and certainly did not attend the delivery. The advice we got from our reading was that at some point the father would be told to go home because the mother-to-be might be quite a long time in labour and the staff didn't need any over-anxious fathers in the way. That we might have been of help to both patient and staff was not a consideration.

We entered the hospital about 10 PM. My wife was moved into a labor room about 11, and I was *not* told to go home; I was told to wait in the fathers' waiting room. There were several others already there. I was not waiting for a baby, but for instructions to go home, get some rest and await a call from the hospital.

We fathers paced, we smoked, we read ancient magazines. We did not talk much. The drill, I soon learned, was that a nurse would come down the hall carrying a baby, call out the father's name, and present the new thing. Around 3 AM there were only two of us left and the other man had just arrived. I heard footsteps in the hall and a baby crying. I knew it had to be mine. I was scared out of my wits. Truly, if there had been a back door to that waiting room, I would have gone out it. I just wasn't ready and I wasn't very wide awake, either. The nurse did her job. She asked which was Mr. Meadow and held out this little creature.

In truth, although she later became a beautiful baby and adult, at first Debra was not much to look at, due to what is called molding, deforming of the skull during passage through the birth canal. Old timers know this effect disappears in a few days to few weeks. I was not an old timer. I did not know. I said to myself that I guess I would love her anyway. As I held her, the predicted feeling came over me. This was something new and, even if scary, it was wonderful. It happened. I was changed. I was a father! Three more children came along for me, Sandra, Alison and Ben. In each case there was instant love, but a first time can only happen once. I could not have foreseen that 24 years after my last child was born another adorable, helpless creature would come into my life.

🐾 🐾 🐾

How does a grown human bond with a four-month old puppy? The obvious things are to play with him, feed him, pet him, train him, and spend lots of time doing these things. Time is important. Dogs demand a lot of attention. As they age they can stand being on their own more and more, but when young they can't. Fortunately, they sleep a lot. So, becoming friends is not hard, just time consuming. But more is needed than friendship. There must be trust, deep trust. The puppy must know that he'll be nourished and protected. I have to know he will trust me, allowing me to handle him in ways others won't be allowed to do. This might mean roughhouse playing or making him take pills or, as we once had to do, applying some medication in the form of salve directly to his eye balls. He, of course, did not know it was medication or that it was good for him. He accepted the indignity calmly. But, he didn't bond with everyone. At the vet's office he is still calm in accepting of the indignities done to him, but while waiting he is very uncomfortable and shivers uncontrollably, something he never does merely from cold temperature.

I mentioned our former dog, Shadow. I did not really know what his mental state was at first, yet within a few days of his coming I was roughhousing with him and found my hand being gently held between his large teeth. At that point I realized I was trusting him not to bite, as he easily could have. And he was big; it would have hurt. He, trusted me in this game. (Big as he was,I was more than twice his weight.) But he had accepted me as the pack leader and I accepted him as a member and we got along from the beginning. Something like that happened between Crispin and me, although because of his youthful inexperience and small size he was never in a position to hurt me. Of the four dogs who have been in our family, it was to him that I came closest.

Dogs are pack animals; in the wild they live in groups, headed by a single leader, called the alpha dog, always a male. There can also be an alpha female, his mate. Lesser members of the pack may be designated by succeeding letters of the Greek alphabet.

I do not know exactly what to do to earn a dog's trust, but they instinctively trust the alpha dog, so an early requirement is to make sure he understands who's who in his pack. I once read (but cannot remember where) that adult mammals will recognize babies of other mammalian species and treat them accordingly. Surely, we humans do that with human babies, kittens, and puppies and recently a friend described the experience of thinking of a baby rhino as cute and lovable, hardly an endearing creature as an adult (figure 10). Young dogs tend to accept handling and leadership from any bigger pack-mate, perhaps justifying that trust we call bonding. The young ones also recognize that there is a leader and learn who it is.

🐕 🐕 🐕

Figure 10. A baby rhinoceros with its mother. Cute? Well maybe, but nothing at all like a two-month old kitten or puppy. Photo © iStockphoto.com/Brad Thompson.

Bonding is not only good for the dog, it is good for the master as well. I remember realizing one day that it was nice to have someone to take care of again, my four children having long since grown up and gone out on their own. No, the dog does not replace children. There are grandchildren but ours do not live close by. However, there are similarities between our relationship with children and pets, but it is not the same. Children grow up to be responsible human adults, we hope. It is the responsibility of the parents to guide them toward that goal. Yes, we have a responsibility to the dog and to the society in which he lives. There should be no biting, excessive barking, or leaving feces on neighbours' lawns. Yes, we get pleasure in watching an ungainly puppy grow and learn and, as an adult, acquire a certain amount of wisdom. But they are not humans. The nature of the love is different. We always know that there is a limit to our joint ability to communicate with and understand one another.

❦ ❦ ❦

What I described so far is more or less Crispin's bonding with me, that is it was mostly a simple matter of his accepting me as alpha. How did I bond with him? After reflecting at length on this question, I decided that the essence of bonding has to be a sense of equality. Of course, I don't mean that Crispin and I are equal in every sense. What I do mean is that there has to be mutual respect and consideration. For him, respect for the alpha is built-in by nature. For the human, it has to mean more than providing for life's needs. Even an enlightened slave owner would have provided those, if only to protect his investment.

A quality of most dogs is loyalty, for life. Do most humans feel that way toward their dog? Do we get rid of the dog because the new condo we cherish won't admit them? Do we leave our dog in the car overnight when staying at a motel that won't admit pets or do we keep looking until we find one that will?

Border Collies, originating in the north of England or Scotland, know all sorts of whistles or hand codes as well as English speech. I have never met a shepherd who works with one of those fabulous dogs. But, clearly, the bond between shepherd and dog is far more than that of boss and assistant. The dog would do anything for the man and I am sure the feeling is mutual.

❦ ❦ ❦

Edgar Prado was the jockey who rode the ill-fated horse Barbaro to a great win in the Kentucky Derby of 2006, only to see him pull up lame in his next race, and eventually die of the ailment caused by the injury. Below are a number of quotations from a book Prado wrote.[2] It is the heart-breaking story, not only of the life and death of a noble horse, but of the intense bonding of a man and a horse. It happens also, of course, between people and dogs.

Prado tells us that at one time he did not make friends with the horses he rode – not until he met Barbaro.

> "Racing fans get philosophical and sentimental about various horses and different aspects of the sport, but when you're on the inside, it's a grueling, cutthroat business and there's no room for sentiment or philosophy."

Later, he adds,

> "When you're getting into this business, you learn from experienced 'racetrackers' not to get too attached to any particular horse. That's the first commandment. Be careful, you're told, they'll only break your heart. . . . If you're a jockey, just get on them, get off them, and move on."

Yet, after riding this horse only twice in competition, on the day they were to win the Kentucky Derby, Prado felt, "we were forming a meaningful bond ... I had confidence in him ... [h]e trusted me to guide him with respect." This is hardly the compete lack of sentiment he was supposed to feel. And eventually,

> "[When] Barbaro came along, . . . I found myself breaking that first commandment – and not just breaking it, but shattering it into a thousand little pieces, like a stone tablet that had been hurled to the ground.
> I couldn't just get on Barbaro, get off him, and move on. I loved him too much.
> It wasn't just that he had done so much for me. It was the way he came to me when he saw me, ears pricked, anxious to communicate. It was the warm look in his eyes when he heard my voice. It was his sense of humor, the way he teased me. . . ."

As for this bonding and love business, I don't know what these are. I do know that the leader of the pack gets his job by being bigger and stronger than any of the others and by protecting the rest of us and seeing that we are fed. The other members of the pack learn to provide respect and obedience, or else. My pack leaders like to pet me, which is nice. I respond by licking them, which shows them I grew up knowing it is a sign of respect, both gladly given and insisted upon. I hope they find that nice. I follow them around; I like to be with them, and a dog is only a member of one pack. Is that what's meant by bonding?

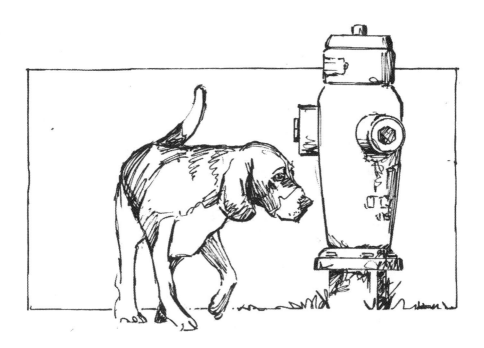

5 The Process of Elimination

WHEN WE GOT Crispin we lived in an apartment in downtown Toronto with, fortunately, a small park only a block away. I have no recollection of how we got through that first day, elimination wise, but the next morning we knew we should get him outside as quickly as possible. We didn't make it. We got half way to the elevator when a small puddle appeared. I have four children; cleaning up the results of elimination was not new or particularly bothersome – well, after the first few times anyway. This hallway experience was the last indoor one, barring illness.

For very young puppies or other mammals, Mama disposes of the infant's waste by licking the appropriate parts. Once the youngster gets beyond as little as a week old, he is on his own in this respect. Pups have an instinct not to foul the nest where they live and Mama helps enforce this. A second point – you can train a dog to "go" outside or on a newspaper in the home, but not both. A choice must be made rather quickly. Since Crispin was four months old when we got him, his mother had made the "where" decision – outside – and had done the dirty work of enforcing the new discipline. All we needed to do was get him outside often enough and everything worked out smoothly. What a relief! (Pun intended.) At first it was four times a day, now merely three.[1]

Now we need to get clinical. How does he show his need and go about his business? We learned more about this after we moved from Toronto to a house with a back yard in Victoria. We found that if he wants to go out, he simply sits by the door. If no one comes he may bark a bit. When released, he could go out, chase birds or squirrels, or just run around. We quickly learned that he will not poo on his own turf. That must be a residual from Mom's insistence on not fouling the nest. Move a few houses away on a walk and he's ready to go. We think he will pee on home territory, but I have never actually seen this happen.

We all know, from comics if nowhere else, that dogs are attracted to fire hydrants. Actually, it is any vertical surface that attracts them. The point of peeing is partly to empty the bladder but even more to mark boundaries. Messages are being sent to another dog. If the dog doing the sniffing detects the odour of another dog on that surface, hydrant, telephone pole, etc., he has to overwrite the previous message, "This area is mine now." or at least, "I've been here." This is more important for male dogs than females. Males are the ones instinctively charged with protecting the territory. That's why males do it by lifting a leg – getting the message higher off the ground where others can read it. That's also why female dogs don't lift their legs to pee; they don't have to do the security work.[2]

If you're a dog and are going to pee on a pole, from which side do you do it? Other than having some physical obstruction in the way, human logic suggests it doesn't matter. But, it seems to matter to Crispin. I often see him sniff at a tree or bush, decide to overwrite the previous dog's marking, move so his leg is in place, say left. Then he turns around and does it instead from the starboard side. It could as well start and end the opposite way. Why? I don't know. One time I saw him start on the right side, switch to left, then back to right, and finally back to left before he proceeded with his business. Ah, well, *chaque à chacun*. Another peculiarity is that after a while, he seems to have emptied his bladder, but it does not stop his marking motions.

🐕 🐕 🐕

If the pee process is so complicated, how about the poo process? To get the pooing done, he has to be outside, away from home. This means a walk, on a leash, or in Toronto a visit to the fairly close off-leash park. Here is where we see some subtlety in the processes. He must select a suitable area. Grass is the much preferred medium, although if we are walking downtown where there is naught but concrete, he seems content to go wherever and whenever the urge occurs. It seems he is thinking there is no proper place to go on grass or dirt, so no point looking – just get on with it. On his preferred medium, he is a practitioner of *feng shui*. The spot must be exactly right. When he has found a suitable area, of perhaps a couple of square meters, he walks deliberately around the patch to find that spot. Then he assumes the position – boy and girl dogs do this the same way – and proceeds. When finished, he moves slightly away and kicks at the grass with his hind legs. Cats do something like this to bury the evidence. Darwin felt that, for dogs, the habit was handed down from previous generations of wolves and dogs and the purpose of the action was long forgotten – so it remains an empty gesture. Morris and Budiansky insist that the reason is not to cover up the evidence, but to spread the dog's odour around. Dogs do love to announce their presence.[3]

The final step is up to the human. We all carry a supply of plastic bags and must immediately step forward to pick up the deposit. This is done by putting the hand into the bag so it is now a glove, doing the pick-up, and then everting the glove so it resumes its role as a bag. All clean and simple. I did not hear this myself, but understand that on a Jerry Seinfeld show he told of an alien invader who came to earth with orders to explore and report. Upon his return home he was asked about the fauna and what kind seemed to be in charge. He described the royalty as four-legged, fur-covered creatures ranging from a third to a full meter high. They were followed around by a much bigger, two-legged servant whose job it was to clean up any mess the smaller one had deposited. If this makes you think that maybe dogs run this planet, you may be right. It really is an interesting comment on how close "man's best friend" has come to being just that in recent years.

One more complication. In a large, cleared area, such as a park, he tends to go off by himself to poo, although he will do the job in full view of anyone – human or dog. One of his walking companions then must go to the spot to clean up, but may miss it. I have more than once found the spot with my foot rather than my eyes, especially in the dark. To counter this, a small flashlight is standard equipment for an evening dog walker.

> People make a big fuss about peeing and pooing. I guess my mom did, too. I wonder why. Do you people make as much fuss when you do it?

Don't underestimate the importance of knowing who has been in your neighbourhood recently and the need to let any intruders know that you live here. You have your ways of protecting yourselves and we have ours.

6 Friends, Strangers, and Noise

REMEMBER THAT Crispin was born and spent his earliest days on a small farm in a rural town. Noise was not much of an issue in his life. We lived downtown in a big city. A block away, on King Street, there was a streetcar line and although city people don't think of these as particularly noisy, Crispin was quite frightened by them at first. Front Street, which our apartment overlooked, was only moderately busy, but there was a fire house about two blocks away. Walking on the street when one of those huge trucks went by with sirens and horns blaring used to drive me crazy, Crispin even more so as a young pup. His typical reaction to these noises was to try to hide. He did the same when we were out walking and he suddenly faced what seemed a throng of people coming at him. It surprised me how quickly he adapted to these noises and crowds. Within about a month he was no longer bothered by fire trucks and streetcars, and actually seemed unaware of their presence. Crowds still bother him a bit, but not seriously.

> It was hard getting used to noises like none I had ever heard before. I'm not sure how or why I got used to some of the worst and I know I still don't like motorcycles. Maybe it's the higher pitched noise than what comes from cars or trucks. I don't like riding in cars, either.

During these early days, he showed no comprehension of what a car was, as long as it made no appreciable noise. This is hardly surprising. Yet, it posed a danger to him because when we came to a street crossing, an approaching car was not a deterrent to him. To this day I do not know what he thinks these various road machines are. He does shy at an approaching baby stroller on the sidewalk, but that is directly in his path. Are they animals? What else moves like that? Since a stroller is pushed by a human, he may see the combination as an extra large human, therefore worth moving away from. But why, then, did he ignore approaching cars when crossing the street? Maybe he did not see or smell any animal connection.

The subway is a highly efficient means of transport in a large city. For the humans, it is easy to use; walk or ride down stairs, wait on a lighted platform until the train arrives and then, when the doors open and are clear, walk in, maybe even find a seat. It will be warm and dry in winter, cool in summer. For a dog, there are problems. The platform may be crowded and people tend to be in a hurry and less inclined to watch out for dogs. When the train arrives it is, to a small dog, a gigantic and very loud machine. That's bad enough. Then it stops, doors open and a herd of people comes pouring out. Then, the herd in which we have been standing pours in. The very last thing a reasonable dog wants to do is follow a crowd. Getting a youthful Crispin to become a willing passenger was not easy. Nothing special was required, just patience. Before too long, he was a regular commuter; on and off like the rest of them.

Figure 11. Dog's eye view of a subway train entrance. It can be crowded enough when you are at the same height as everyone else, but when all you see are legs and feet it can be a frightening experience. Photo © iStockphoto/ Enviromantic.

🐾 🐾 🐾

Once we got over the road noise problem, it was time to start the process of dealing with people other than the immediate family. This turned out to be no trouble. He is shy at the start but may take only a minute to warm up to a person, less if there is a treat involved. He learned early to get very excited at a knock or ringing at our front door. He barks furiously and runs to the door, but he pays no attention to a telephone ringing. Also, however excited he may get at the doorbell sound, he immediately accepts almost anyone that a member of the household allows in. But, let a stranger be unexpectedly found in his territory and he vigorously defends either the turf, himself, or ourselves – to this day we are not sure which it is. That word *almost* three lines back will be elaborated on in chapter 14.

Getting along with other dogs is variable, depending on the circumstances. I have to look ahead here to December 2002 and January 2003 when, within a 30-day period he was attacked and badly bitten by two different dogs, both large and mainly black. Ever since, he has been wary of any such dog and sometimes any dog at all who is bigger than he is. However, in a normal situation, when he is off leash, he is every dog's friend, big or small, black or white.

> Yes, those fights with the two dogs still bother me. I was just minding my own business when suddenly one of them was on me, too big for me to do much about it. With the first one I tried to give up, which dogs usually do when they know they can't win, but he ignored me and bit anyway. The second one attacked from the rear. I never saw it coming. I do know that a dog bites in the back of the neck when he really wants to kill. We don't usually do that to each other

Near our home in Toronto was a park, roughly one city block in size. The city's rule was that dogs could be there off leash for a few hours in the early morning and again in the evening. Actually, they were only allowed to use half the park; the other half had a rarely used softball diamond and sometimes soccer players used the whole park. A map was posted that showed the dog area in red. As many as twenty dogs might convene there of an evening and there was never any real fighting. They had their favorites but no enemies. Dogs, of course, do not read maps or signs intended for humans. They were cheerfully oblivious of any restrictions on themselves in the park and we were not able to teach them to accept a boundary in the middle of a continuous grassy field. I did have some initial success teaching Crispin not to go onto the abutting sidewalk, that is to stay on the grass. The mixtures of both dogs and people in this park was fascinating. We had mongrels and kennel club registrants, hundred-pound-plus dogs and Chihuahuas, and people from all walks of life, but sharing a love for dogs.

Crispin quickly found a girl friend. Her name was Elska. She was about his age, a mix of Pomeranian and Maltese and very cute. Once they got to know each other, each would make a bee line for the other when they were both in the park together. Elska's owner hoped to let her have one litter and hoped Crispin might be the father. Alas, it was too late. The surgeon's knife had done its work.

In our apartment building, down the hall from us lived a Sheltie named Jake. These two also became close friends, but they were two

Figure 12. This is Elska, grown up now and mother of her own pups. Ah, but in their youth she and Crispin were quite an item. Photo courtesy of her owner, Kirsten Bishopric

guys, no romance. It was interesting. They rarely played together but both enjoyed the company of the other. They just liked being together. Crispin would often leave the elevator and go directly to Jake's door, rather than his own. They could be taken on walks together but they had different preferences for how and where to walk. It took some skill to keep them together.

> Ah, Elska. A nice girl. Jake was nice, too. but there was a difference. I'm not sure why I'm attracted to females but do know it felt nicer with her.

❖

There are other animals than dogs and people, of course. If it's a small animal, cat, mouse, squirrel, raccoon, sometimes even a bird, Crispin's Terrier instincts come into play. He would love to catch one, but with one exception never has. The one time was while visiting a house in Southern California which had a family of what were called tree rats living in the back yard. These apparently are not as offensive as those found farther north, but humans have their instincts, too, and we tend to grow up with an abhorrence of rats. Crispin did his duty, but instead of killing his prey he played cat and mouse with it. I had to finish the poor creature off. It was, and remains, the largest animal I have ever killed.

I don't know where this desire to play with a captured animal comes from. It seems very cruel. Our cat Max once caught a mouse in our house and did this rather than dispatch him. I, who had tried to get Max to catch the beast, couldn't bear to watch. I took the mouse outside and let him go. He was in a catatonic state I thought that if he made it, good for him. If not, there was nothing I could do. A day later he was gone forever

When play fighting with other dogs Crispin was quite spirited. If the other dog was much bigger, that dog would, of course, win easily.

But Crispin would get up quickly and go right back at the other guy. That feisty spirit seems to be built into Terriers, whether this was stressed in human selective breeding or naturally developed to make them good at their appointed jobs. But feistiness can go to extremes. One day in Toronto he encountered a horse for the first time, actually two large horses ridden by two large policemen. Crispin went at them like Don Quixote going for a windmill. He barked and acted very aggressively, but did not get close enough to bite. The cops laughed and just warned me to keep him from behind the horses whose kicks, of course, could be fatal. Today, the only horses he sees in Victoria are pulling carriages loaded with tourists. Occasionally he barks; he usually just disdains them. Don Quixote would have approved. Such non-warrior class horses are beneath the dignity of a true knight.

Figure 13. These are the kind of horses that were the first such animals Crispin ever saw. He was ready for battle since they were encroaching on his turf (a public park). The good natured officers simply warned me to be careful of Crispin getting kicked. Photo from Metropolitan Toronto Police.

Figure 14. This handsome fellow pulls carriages for a living. Crispin first saw such a horse two years after he first saw the police horses. By then he had no reason to object to the presence of a mere working horse, not worthy of combat with a noble dog. Photo by C. Meadow.

Horses, in a way, remind me of trucks, but I have learned, mostly by smell, that they are animals not machines. The first two I met seemed very threatening, but ever since the ones I see do not seem interested in bothering me, so I don't bother them, much.

7 Dominance, Separation, and Aggression

DOG USERS' MANUALS warn about dogs and dominance, that is dogs who want to be the alpha or at least beta of their dog-human pack. As Crispin got older, he did seem to feel he was responsible for security of the pack (see chapter 13) or to have his own way on walks. However, he never showed any tendency to dominate in such ways as insisting that he go through doors first, or that he had the sole right to sit next to the alpha member. I did know one owner who described that latter habit exactly. Her dog would insert himself between her and her husband when sitting on the couch. They allowed the dog to sleep in their bed, but I never knew her well enough to explore the rather obvious next question.

Generally, Crispin shows the opposite of intent to dominate Mary Louise or me. He treats us almost as equals, obeys either of us, looks for affection from either of us, and gives to us equally. That word *al-*

most will be addressed in chapter 13. It has to do with his feeling that she still needs his protection. Whenever we three are outside, walking together and one of the humans goes off in a different direction, as to enter a store or go on to the office, he is clearly bothered. Usually, he sits down and stares at the departing one or even at the door through which he or she has gone. It can be a bit of a struggle to get him started moving again. It makes no difference which of us leaves the scene.

Is his upset over one of us leaving the pack separation anxiety? I do not know. I do know that when we leave him with someone else, outside our home, such as a kennel or friend's house, he may have a good time but he gets very excited at the reunion. He shakes all over, wags his tail furiously, and runs back and forth between Mary Louise and me, wanting to be petted vigorously. It's almost worth leaving him for the joy of the reunion. There will be more about this, called greeting behaviour, and its meaning in chapters 10 and 18.

> Don't forget we like being part of a pack. To suddenly find there is no pack around you is frightening. I'm pretty calm about it but I know of other dogs who are not. And yes, I am glad to see you get back. Maybe some part of the greeting is to hint that you shouldn't go away.

How bad a problem is separation anxiety? It can be awful. Cats may scratch the antique furniture or defecate on the oriental rugs. Dogs may chew or knock things down. It does no good to say, "We love you and we'll be back soon" as you're leaving the house. They will want company or at least comfort. We sometimes leave a radio playing for Crispin, but it does not really seem to have an effect. He is pretty good if left for short periods and we rarely leave him for long periods. "Long" is perhaps four hours or more. We can go safely to a movie or out to dinner. He usually just goes to sleep. I do not know if we did anything particularly right to achieve this behaviour by Crispin except perhaps that he gets lots of attention when we're home.

🐕 🐕 🐕

I began to notice that other, older dogs, if restrained by a leash, could be rather aggressive when another dog passed by. In Toronto, we had a number of restaurants nearby that had tables outside. You could see the most peaceful looking dog being held close to its owner's chair but as another dog walked by there were threatening noises from the restrained one. We see this even from dogs locked in a car when another dog walks by and on occasion a dog in a moving car might bark aggressively at a dog on the sidewalk. As Crispin grew up, and to this day, he may do the same. The most common theory of this behaviour among owners is that the dog feels frightened because he is constrained and could not fight if it were necessary. Hence, they adopt aggressive behaviour to frighten the other dog away. Dogs, anyway mentally healthy dogs, do not necessarily want to fight. They almost always make noises and gestures to intimidate the other dog so that withdrawal of the latter from the field of combat is the better course. More on this in chapter 18.

A second theory is that the dog, knowing his owner has him thoroughly in check, is free to show off as much as he wants, with no danger the owner will allow him to engage in actual combat.

Professional trainers tend to feel that the dog senses that the person leading him is worried about an approaching meeting and feels it necessary to protect his pack-mate. One solution is to subtly move your dog out of the path of the on-coming dog and avoid conflict. Another is to convince him you are not worried or that you are in charge, not the dog. I do this by kneeling down, one hand on his chest (to limit movement) and talk quietly as the other dog approaches. This usually pacifies the other dog, too. Several times, I have simply dropped the leash as we approached a questionable dog and no trouble resulted. On the other hand, if the on-coming dog still looks like he is planning trouble, either Crispin responds in kind or we try to get him away before anything can happen. He may respond aggressively to another dog regardless of their relative sizes. I guess that's the Terrier gene in him.

> Us dogs know that we may have to fight sometimes to protect our turf or our pack. Sometimes, threats are enough. They are always preferred. Why fight when you can convince the other guy he is going to lose?

Now, we are a family who are accepting of all sorts of people who are different from us, and we're pretty well mongrelized ourselves. So it was with surprise that I began to notice a streak of racism in Crispin, not with respect to people, but for or against other breeds of dogs. Ever since his first attack by a Black Lab, whenever he meets almost any large dark-coloured dog, his demeanor varies from mistrust to naked hostility. This, at least is understandable, but it does not happen when he is off leash. There is a similar problem with Beagles who, more often than not, initiate the problem. Except for those two attacks, I have never seen him actually engaged in combat with any dog, but he does carry out that intimidation act to the max. On the other hand, he tends to like dogs smaller than himself and usually recognizes puppies as such and tolerates their puppy-like behaviour, to a point. Some puppies are bigger than he is by age three months and, when they get frisky and want to wrestle, he is very much bothered, but avoids fighting. If they are frisky but not too domineering, he may play for a few seconds, then just back off, in effect saying, "You play. I'll just watch."

One the good side, Golden Retrievers always get a good reception from him, as do Schnauzers, Wheaten Terriers and Chihuahuas. In the dog parks we frequented in Toronto and Victoria there were lots of Golden Retrievers, always friendly, so he always treats them well. Does his parentage bring out some knowledge of his own genetic make up? Or does he just recognize from the smell that Schnauzers and Wheatens are superior beings?

There are some dogs who become special friends and there are some that make it plain they are likely to cause trouble, as those two big dogs once did. As for the Beagles, the first one I ever met starting snarling and barking at me, so I answered in kind, at him or any that looked like him. Don't tell me you humans don't do the same thing. And yes, I do recognize Schnauzers and Wheatens as relatives. None has ever done me any harm or threatened to. Same with Golden Retrievers. I've known quite a few of them and they've always been nice.

8 Socializing

"Socialize," the book said. Obediently, when Crispin was still quite young I began to take him to all sorts of places – stores, banks, offices, meetings, even classes. I was astounded at his behaviour. Always perfect, angelic. It was as if he had been previously well trained in how to behave in someone else's domain.

Of course, angelic behaviour is for angels and Crispin is a dog. As I said earlier, we lived in an apartment house when we first got him. At our end of our floor were three families, so not much traffic walking by. But due to some defect in our fire alarm system, we had frequent false alarms. A bell would ring fiercely. People would begin walking down stairs to evacuate, and there was a door to one flight near our apartment door. Crispin did not like the bell or the sounds of strangers going by our door and he let everyone know it by loud barking. Then, he seemed to like that and would bark whenever a stranger walked in front of our door, whether coming home or visiting a neighbour. The resident across the hall we hardly ever saw and the noise did not seem to have much effect. Next door, though, lived good friends one of whom did not much care to be yelled at for the crime of coming home. Fortunately, he seemed to value our friendship more than he resented Crispin, so we all survived this. One night when we were having one of our false alarms a resident on another floor had trouble with his or her medical oxygen supply and an ambulance was summoned. The Emergency Medical Technicians avoided the elevator as we were always instructed, and made a fair amount of noise going past our door on the way to the stairs. Crispin barked loudly and long. I have a feeling that normally so much noise might have gotten us a reprimand from the condominium council.

Another incident of non-angelic behaviour occurred when, in the interest of socialization, I took him to the apartment of some friends where we had to do some work together. Crispin was, at first and as usual, an angel. But I had been working with the lady of the house and when her husband came home Crispin, apparently deciding that this was now his turf, barked as he did when strangers came to our own door. No physical harm was done, but the gentleman, like my neighbour, was not one to appreciate being yelled at in his own house, especially by a dog.

> As I said before, I am a pretty friendly guy when I do not feel threatened. The tough stuff happens when I do feel that way. My owners often can't understand what it is that threatens me. When we go to strange places, I usually feel comfortable but that doesn't mean I never feel threatened in the new place. More often than not, in a strange place, I go to sleep.

Crispin was and is no dummy. He made good friends with all the apartment house staff, especially with one of the night concierge-security men. John apparently lived alone and he loved dogs but did not have one of his own. When Crispin came in the door or out of the elevator, John would jump up, greet him like a valued resident, and play with him. If John offered his hand for a shake. Crispin raised his paw and John shook it and grinned. He was convinced he taught Crispin how to do this. I didn't have the heart to tell him that I thought what was happening was that Crispin was pulling his paw away, which required lifting it, not offering it. Anyway, they got along famously and I think John was heart broken when we moved away.

In a typical visiting environment, Crispin does some quick exploring, then, realizing he is not involved in any action and isn't going to be fed, he goes to sleep.

He has learned that some (in his mind all) stores give free treats. The stimulus seems to be a counter. If there is one, to him it is natural law that behind it is or will soon be a person who will give him a treat. After a single such experience, he will never willingly walk past that store without going in. I am pleasantly surprised at how many shops recognize him, or recognize that all dogs behave this way, and cheerfully give a treat even if we are not buying anything.

Figure 15. Crispin and his friend John shake hands. Photo by C. Meadow.

An opposite pattern is exhibited when we go to a veterinary office. There is our regular one and an emergency hospital. In both, he quickly realizes where he is, walks toward the door and waits to go out. Obviously, he is restrained from doing so. In an examining room, he is passively cooperative but shivers as a sign of fear. One time I took him to our auto dealership whose waiting room is similar to any medical waiting room, except for more up to date magazines and free coffee and cookies. Even so, he shivered, perhaps in fear that they were going to change his oil, too.

🐾 🐾 🐾

All told, we feel that Crispin is a well socialized dog who can be trusted in most situations and, for example, taken into any store or office willing to accept him. As you'll see in Chapter 14, on security, there are exceptions.

Am I afraid of new people? Not always, but a smart dog has to size up potential enemies. Hardly any dog starts fighting right away. There is usually a period of sizing up, then if necessary, some growling or barking, and only then an attack if the other guy won't back away. Being nice for a few seconds doesn't prove anything. I do not "shake hands" with strangers and I do it with my pack leader sometimes to please him, but it does not please me. I particularly do not like strangers to touch me on top of my head or to wiggle their fingers before my eyes. So, if they are friendly to me, I am friendly to them.

Those doctors are not very nice. I do not like the way I am handled and poked by them.

9 Obedience School and Lifelong Learning

THE NEXT STEP, after initial bonding and socializing, is obedience school. The first lesson in obedience school is that this is a school for owners, not dogs. *They* do not teach your dog obedience, *you* do. They teach you how to do it, and there's homework. Our instructor had a Border Collie, a dog noted for high intelligence in the sense of willingness and ability to learn. Whatever he was asked to do, he did immediately and perfectly. To some of us, he represented the ultimate objective – if only *my* dog could learn to do all that. To me, this brought to mind a quotation from Thomas Jefferson, who, when ambassador to France from the infant United States, wrote, "I like a little rebellion now and then."[1] No, he was not a closet anarchist, he was a believer in independence and recognized that being independent was not consistent with always doing exactly what you are told. I felt the same about my children. Yes, I wanted them to be well behaved, but *perfectly* behaved meant, to me, lacking in a spirit of independence and creativity. I thought I'd like my dog to be like that – a little spirit, obedient but with a mind of his own even if it meant trouble now and then. What I did not know at the time was that I was thinking of dogs in general, not Terriers in general, and certainly not Crispin in particular. Terriers tend to come with a built in independent, stubborn streak.

🐾 🐾 🐾

School consisted of our teaching the dogs some basic commands and the instructor teaching us how to teach the dogs. The two most important things I learned had to do with voice tone and rewards. Rewards were food, and maybe a pat on the back and some nice words, but nothing works like food. The instructor used the expression "Flood them with food." Not just one treat, a stream of them. The voice tone points he made were interesting. Dogs like soft, high pitched voices. Give commands as you would a small child and start with the dog's name: "Crispin, sit." This in a high tone, sounding as sweet as you can make it. If there is resistance, step up to a more authoritative tone. Do not get harsh with the dog, especially when commanding him to come. A harsh toned "Come" makes the dog realize he is in trouble and there is no point coming just to get punished. All this was good advice, it keeps on working.

Crispin was not a star performer but both he and I learned a few things. He learned to sit on command. He learned to lie down on a combination of a command and a hand gesture. He learned the critically important command, COME. He learned it his way. What you want the dog to do is immediately come to where you are and await a next command, probably SIT. What I often get is a silent message, "I hear you. I'll be there when I'm ready. Don't hold your breath."

The main thing I learned was that dogs will do anything for food. So, the way COME works with us is, I call out "Come" and wave a dog biscuit at him. His spirit of independence now tells him to come a runnin'. So much for integrity.

The other side of this if-there's-food-I-surrender behaviour is that dogs are remarkably loyal. Once bonded with a pack, he's a member for life except perhaps in case of very bad treatment. He may play his little game with COME, but he is not about to run away. A recommended response to delay or refusal to come is not to chase him, but to walk away, then sneak a look over your shoulder and see him running to you.

> Obedience school wasn't much fun. Too many dogs and people in a small building, all kinds of nervous dogs. There were too many people insisting that we do funny kinds of things. But there was a lot of good food. And speaking of good, there was a goody-goody dog that lived there, always showing off how he obeyed all the commands. He seemed to have no mind of his own.

There were other things he needed to learn in his young life and I needed to learn about him. One of these was walking down stairs. Back in his first home in Terra Cotta, he lived on the ground floor of a barn. Stairs were not part of his life. Going up a stairway is easy; he can plainly see what's in front of him. Down was a new experience. When he first looked down a flight of stairs, what we think he saw was a long, steep ramp, not a series of easy steps. He did not want to get on it. Here is where my obedience training came in handy. The thing to do was get below him on the stairs, encourage him to take one step down, which he did not want to do, but hold out a treat in the form of a cube of cheese. Hold the cheese just below where he is. As I said before, he'll do anything for food, so down a step he would come. Do it again, another step. Not too many times in one day. It took about a week and a half pound of cheese but ever since the lesson has stuck. He no longer fears stairs. Indeed, in our present house he rarely walks up or down stairs; he runs.

🐾 🐾 🐾

In Toronto and many other cities, especially downtown, there are many metal grates embedded in the sidewalks. Just outside our Toronto apartment house door there was one. Under it was a deep empty space, then a window of some sort into a machinery room, probably for the air conditioner system to blow away hot air. The combination of noise, vibration, and the unpleasant feeling of stepping on this grate with bare feet bothered him greatly. (Sorry, another pun, not intended.) He would simply freeze before it, refuse to move. Gradually we taught him it was possible to walk around the grate, but he has to be led to it. Victoria has fewer of these things but there are some. To this day, he does not simply go around one on his own, although he sometimes jumps over a small one.

🐾 🐾 🐾

We managed to convince him, surprisingly easily, that he is not permitted on our antique sofa or our bed. In regard to this training, I learned something. When training a dog not to do something, what he learns is not to get caught doing it. I leave it to the reader to imagine what the difference is. If you're having trouble seeing what I mean, think back to your childhood and remember what you did when forbidden to do something by your parents.

🐾 🐾 🐾

I pointed out earlier that I am not a professional dog trainer or anything close. Did I rate an A in obedience training? No. There remained two behaviours I could hardly make an inroad on. The first has to do with the front door. When the bell rings or someone knocks, he goes crazy, barks furiously, and shakes all over. I know what we were once told to do – get someone or some people to come to the door, ring the bell and just wait. When he starts barking, we should make some unpleasant noise, such as shaking a tin can with a few rocks or pennies in it. Do this over and over. Gradually, he will break his habit of that raucous behaviour. But, it takes time and we really need a bell ringer whose presence he cannot recognize. So sloth has won and until recently we still had the noisy reaction. One session with Dr. Mary Ann Leason, a psychologist, using only positive rein-forcement – help the dog *want* to do what you ask – almost immediately offered hope that this situation is curable.

The second unpleasant behaviour is his aggressiveness on meeting some other dogs while on a walk. The problem here is that he is statistically more likely to be friendly than not, so it is hard to antici-pate which approaching dog might trigger the bad reaction. I certainly don't want to train him to avoid all other dogs. We had attended some training classes with Dr. Leason on this issue, with some improvement, but not yet total. And, there is always the problem that half the time it's the other dog who starts the trouble.

🐕 🐕 🐕

We moved from Toronto to Victoria, British Columbia, when Crispin was two years old. Here, and in some other cities, dogs must be leashed in public spaces other than designated dog parks unless the dog is "under control." That means the person in charge has to be able to demonstrate that the dog will come at once when called. The best example is to watch any Border Collie when called, which puts the owners of most other dogs to shame. Crispin has to stay on leash.

Leashes come in two styles. One is about two meters in length, made of leather, metal chain, or nylon fabric. The other is much longer and winds up on a retractable spool, like a fishing reel. Either is attached to the dog's collar or harness. The collar is a simple, small belt-like object that goes around the neck. The harness has one part that goes around the neck and one that goes around the top of the body, behind the forelegs. The two parts are connected. All this is to point out that the fixed-length leash connected to a neck collar means that if either the person in charge or the dog pulls hard, the dog gets choked, obviously a most uncomfortable feeling. To counter this, there is a Gentle Leader® – a loop of leather or fabric that goes around the snout instead of around the neck. A very gentle, painless tug sends the dog a signal of direction to turn, stop, or do something he knows is expected of him. And if he really pulls, it still doesn't hurt, while Crispin with the conventional connection of leash-to-neck-collar would often cause some pain to himself. Crispin wears one of these. People often stop me on the street asking why such a cute, peaceful-looking dog is muzzled. I explain the function, then add that he can still bite if he wants to. I get strange looks from adding that bit about biting, and often watch the questioner back cautiously away.

What has all this to do with learning? Crispin hates to have the gentle lead put on. Stanley Coren, who researches and writes on dog behaviour, says that an adult dog has about the same intelligence as a two-year old human child.[2] Picture such an intelligent child being faced with having a snowsuit put on. This is where passive resistance was invented. It is also an exact description of Crispin when he sees the dreaded lead coming toward him, in my hands. He will back away, run away, or if cornered, turn his head to make it harder to attach the beast. If it weren't frustrating, it would be funny. There is no way I can think of to get across to him that this is for his benefit.

However, as I write this, I realize I should have been feeding him a treat every time I was about to put the leader on him. So, the failure is mine.

🐕 🐕 🐕

Learning, as almost any university advertises these days, is a lifelong thing. What they mean is you should register for a continuing education course, which does wonders for the university's income. But, it also happens to be a valid statement. It applies to dogs as well as people. Long after school was formally over for him, I taught some new things or he learned them by himself.

Stop at a street crossing. He is to stop, then sit and await the command, GO. I do not remember when he learned STOP because I never consciously taught it, but he quickly learned the sequence STOP, SIT, GO. Each time he sat, he got a treat. He was to remain sitting until released by GO. I wanted to do this for two reasons. One was safety. He still lacks a sense of an automobile as danger, so crossing a street with him was like crossing with that two-year old child in tow. You can't let the child decide when it is safe to go. The second reason was to reinforce who was in charge of the walk. Crispin had gradually tended to want to dictate the pace and direction of a walk. Sometimes that is OK, but he needed to learn that this was a privilege, not a right. Now, he almost always sits automatically as we approach a crossing point. The command to do so is not needed. It's "almost" because he is easily distracted and, if there is anything interesting going on at or near the corner, he forgets his duty and must be reminded.

It took me some time to realize that while Crispin is quite good at stopping and sitting, and he normally waits for a GO before getting up and moving, he actually has a broader range of signals he accepts as meaning GO. He will sometimes get up upon hearing anything spoken to him after he sits. Also, he gets up and goes if anyone waiting with him moves forward. This does not have to be myself or Mary Louise. It can be any other person waiting at the same traffic light. That seemed another good lesson to anyone training anyone else, be it dog or child. Be aware of what you have actually taught the learner as the signal to do something. It may not be what you intended him to learn.

Tolerate strangers playing with him. For his first three or four years, Crispin was not comfortable with strangers touching him, especially patting his head or, as small children often do, wiggling fingers in front of his face. Whether it is something he learned or merely old age creeping in, he is far more tolerant today. He ducks away from a strange hand over his head but does not snap at the fingers.

Mealtime. It was not until he was four or five years old that he got used to the "signals" that meant breakfast or dinner is being prepared. These are not intentional on our part, they are the noises made in preparing his meal or even setting his dish down on the floor. He has lately begun looking for the food around his usual feeding times.

There is an after dinner ritual, too. We usually eat dinner early and afterwards adjourn to the living room to watch the six o'clock news on the American PBS channel. When Crispin sees this migration, he knows it is time for his treats and he rushes ahead of us and assumes the sitting position which is his signal that he expects to get a post-prandial treat.

We have heard of dogs who seem to know the time of day and begin bugging the owners when to provide dinner. It is, of course, possible that they hear or see something that tells them the humans are preparing food, but most owners from whom I hear this claim it is that time alone is the stimulus and as mentioned above, recently, we have seen this behaviour at about 5 PM.

Some improvement in coming. I described Crispin's behaviour when he is off leash and either Mary Louise or I approach him with leash in hand, ready to go home. He used to go, and sometimes still does, into a catch-me-if-you-can mode. He will sit, lie down, sometimes make the play bow (see chapter 16 about this), then as we get within about a meter, he gets up and runs farther away. Although many believe that dogs don't really smile (see chapter 19 about this), he always seems to be doing just that when playing this game. I think he is avoiding the leash, not the going home. Of late, if we walk back to the car, he follows. We open the door, he hops in without being told or resisting, no leash involved. Nice feeling of relief on our parts.

🐕 🐕 🐕

Crispin is eight years old as I write this and we have reached a point where he is reasonably obedient, somewhat rebellious, but at a nice balance point, of being both interesting and pleasant to have around.

As to learning after the school ended, of course we keep on learning things. Don't you? I had to learn what my leaders were like, what they wanted of me, how they acted on a walk. I had to learn which dogs I could trust and which not to trust, which stores give treats to dogs and which not.

PART II   Coming of Age

In this part I mostly describe Crispin as an adult dog and see how he outgrows his puppy-like behaviour. A lot of independence, some self-learning, some unpleasant incidents.

10   Around the House

THIS CHAPTER covers eating, sleeping, bathing, asking to go out, and dealing with company. Of these, eating is the number one in importance. The ancestral wolves were northern animals. Food was scarce. One form of food was a large animal, such as a moose, part of a herd walking across the wolves' territory. The usual tactic was to separate a laggard from the rest, then pounce on that one, with a multiple-wolf attack. A moose is much bigger than a wolf, or even a small group of them, and could provide more than one normal meal for them all, but the wolves could not store the carcass away for the next meal, partly because there are other scavengers who would feast on anything left behind. It had to be eaten then and there. That meant they gorged themselves on all they could eat, because the next moose herd would not come on schedule.[1] It's believed that this was the origin of dogs' seemingly unending appetites. This must also have been the origin of the World War II expression, *submarine wolf pack* – a group of submarines hunting together for enemy ships, very effectively.

Unlike at least the popular version of cats' eating habits, dogs do not seem to know the meaning of *enough*. They can eat a good meal, then smell something interesting, and act like they haven't eaten in a week. Our first vet told us that dogs could go about two weeks without food, but nothing like that without water. Wolves are said to be able to last days to weeks without feeding.[2] So Crispin, like other dogs, is always interested in eating. He has learned that a human with a hand in his or her pocket is in that posture for only one reason – to find a treat to give him. This is obviously an error, but common to many dogs. A treat, if it is given by a stranger, is usually a dog biscuit. The protocol of the situation is to ask the dog's owner for permission before giving a gift and if OK, make it small. If he receives such a gift, the dog is instantly ready for another.

Crispin's real meals are given twice a day and consist of two-thirds cup of dry dog food, the concoction called kibble. We usually flavor this with a bit of cheese, gravy, soup, egg, fish, etc. He seems more attracted by the odour than the taste so a little flavouring goes a long way. He became overweight at about age three and has been on diet food ever since. And it works; he was about 7 kgs when we got him, went quickly up to 14 then, with a diet, slowly down to 11 where he should remain. (Note: *should*, not necessarily *does*.)

We have sometimes given him big bones with marrow and perhaps a bit of meat still clinging, to chew on. He loves them. Friends, who dearly love him, will save them for him. Unfortunately, he has shown a tendency to become sick at his stomach after eating such a treat, so they have been banned from his diet. We think this food is just too rich for him. Basically, he is a happy eater and loves nothing so much as an extra snack outside of meal times.

Eating is important and you guys are good feeders. That does not mean that any sensible dog would pass up an opportunity for another snack. How can we be sure when we'll get the next meal?

❧

A very close second to eating is sleeping. It appears that if you're a dog and nothing of any serious interest is going on, you sleep. Crispin usually sleeps through the night but may get up and move to a different bed once or twice. Then there are frequent naps during the day. (Aah, if only I could do that.) He has two modes of waking up, slow and fast. In slow mode, he stands up and begins to stretch slowly, just as cats do. Only then is he ready for the day's activities. In fast mode, if he hears the wrong kind of noise, he is awake instantly and ready for action. What's a wrong noise? Loud, sharp, unexpected, or just unfamiliar. We have not had a burglar since Crispin came to us, but I think he would wake up to even a minor sound in the house that he does not recognize, quickly coupled with the smell of a stranger. Then, watch out! But, this hypothesis has only been tested by outside animal noises

His napping is done in many spots around the house. His favourite is a futon in Mary Louise's office. Next choice is a large recliner chair. If that's not available, he will nap on any other upholstered chair, except for the antique sofa from which he is restricted. He also likes to lie down on the carpeted stairs, especially on hot days.

Sleeping, whether as a nap or for the night, is done in a dazzling array of positions. These are shown figure 16. The normal one is lying on his side. He can do this lying straight or curled up in a way you wouldn't think a vertebrate animal could do. He may also lie on his back, feet up in the air, looking ridiculous but comfortable. Then, there is the prone position, on his belly, forelegs outstretched, snout on the floor between the legs. In the latter position he is usually

Figure 16. Sleeping positions. Top row: Rolled up into a ball; sleeping on his back. Centre: Lying in the prone position. Bottom row: (l) sleeping in a normal, non-contorted position, but (r) sometimes he just likes to withdraw from the world. Photos by C. Meadow.

awake, but quite relaxed. Then, there is a more normal sleep position. The last of them shows something of what he was like when, as a puppy, he was overcome by noise and crowds on the streets of Toronto and needed to retreat from the world but with his eyes open.

At night he settles down when Mary Louise and I do. If we happen to be watching television just before retiring, he takes his cue from it being turned off. Up he gets and follows us upstairs. If no TV is in use, he is likely to be resting on Mary Louise's office futon in a room adjacent to the living room. If so, he has to be awakened and summoned to bed. He settles in our bedroom, where he has his own bedding. He is restricted from our bed. But, he may get up during the night, go down to the living room, to the spare bedroom I use as an office, or to a particularly good stair.

The Monks of New Skete are a community of monks who raise and train dogs and who collectively wrote an excellent book on raising puppies. They recommended that the family dog be allowed in the main bedroom but not in the bed, on the grounds that he considers himself one of the family but shouldn't be a full equal.[3] This made sense to me. However much we love the little dear, he is often dirty and at times may assert himself as the one in charge. It is not a good relationship for the dog to be in charge of the family, or even think he is. It's a little like having a small child. Obviously, the child is a member of the family from day one, but is quite different from other members. The difference between the child and the dog is that the child will grow up to become one like us, but the dog will not.

> What else is there to do but sleep? You read, listen to music, watch TV, or talk to other people. I can't do any of that. With me, it's eat, go out, get someone to play with me, or go to sleep.

Bathing does not fall in the category of favorite things to do. It involves getting water all over him. He does not like baths and he does not like full immersion in water at the beach. We bathe him in the family tub using a hose with a spray nozzle. He hates it. I have to lift him in. In fact as soon as he realizes why I have called him upstairs, he begins to retreat, so I have to pick him up and put him in the tub. Then, I wet him down, one hand on the hose, one holding him in, and apply shampoo. (Of course shampoo. Would we use ordinary soap on our little prince? Actually, it was recommend by a vet, when he had some minor skin problem as a puppy.) He does enjoy being scrubbed. Petting is petting; you take what you can get. He likes the taste of the shampoo, made from oatmeal and aloe and containing no soap. He keeps trying to escape, but it's like getting his gentle lead on him. He resists but only passively. Finally, we're done. He kind of likes drying, another form of petting.

It is very difficult to dry him completely, given his thick mop of fur. So, when we're finished, he runs for the nearest oriental carpet and rolls himself around on it till he feels dry. But, he is capable of getting very dirty and he always looks much better afterward. He never appreciates it.

Ycch.

I mentioned Crispin's response to the doorbell or to a knock on the door. Let's begin a bit earlier. If he hears our garage door opening, he knows it is likely that one of us has come home. We live in a cluster of four town houses, each having a near identical garage door, but ours, of course is closer, hence louder. Does he know which of us is not home? I don't know. I do know that when he hears that sound, he is expectant but not alarmed. For all of his vaunted sense of smell, I

Figure 17. After the bath Crispin's bushy hair almost most disappears, explosing his dark skin below. He looks very forlorn, but recovers as soon as he's released from the tub. Photo by C. Meadow.

do not think he can recognize who is coming before the door opens. I know that if I ring the bell he reacts just as if it were a stranger. But, as before, once the door is opened, the response changes and he is generally accepting. One time, the person coming in was a stranger, here to do some work, and he bent over just inside the door, perhaps to take off his shoes – I didn't actually see this happen. Mary Louise did and says Crispin lunged as if to bite. A few minutes later, he was back to accepting, so it must have been something in the man's body motion that caused the problem. It happens only rarely that someone other than Mary Louise or I will come though the front door without knocking or ringing. It will always be someone we have given a key to and who is known to Crispin. When this happens, he does not bark or raise a fuss. It tends to confirm that his reaction is to the ringing or knocking, not to the person doing it.

Another time, we were bringing Crispin home from having been away for a time. As soon as he entered the house, he made a mad dash through all the rooms. A cousin had stayed in the house while we were away and Crispin could smell him but not find him. This is somewhat comforting behaviour in case of burglars. Our pre-Crispin experience with burglaries was that if the police are called, the first thing they want to do is check to see if the culprit is still in the house. What better way to find out?

Once the callers are in and accepted, Crispin has two modes of dealing with them. One is to ignore everyone and go to sleep. But he is more likely to start by going from seated person to person looking for either food or petting. He will also usually do his greeting behaviour thing, putting his feet on the person's upper leg. This is an act of endearment to dog lovers but two of our friends were dog phobic and this terrified them, although it carried no hostility from Crispin. Well, we knew it was benignly intended and Crispin knew that, but these guests didn't care. They hated and feared it.

If eating is involved, as it usually is when there is company, he follows us to the table and makes the rounds. He is not fed from the table but this does not at all seem to dampen his hopes.

With people he has known before, Crispin can be a gracious host. He shows his recognition and welcome by this greeting behaviour. Charles Darwin described this in a book published in 1872. Before finding this book, I used to think of Crispin's greetings as unique. But Darwin knew about it way back then. He began by describing a dog out walking, seeing a man approaching whom he first thought was a stranger. Hence, he (the dog) assumed a position that goes with hostility and preparation for fighting. But, then he recognized the man as his master and his mood changed radically, as Darwin described it.

> [T]he body sinks downwards or even crouches, and is thrown into flexuous movements; his tail, instead of being held stiff and upright, is lowered and wagged from side to side; his hair instantly becomes smooth; his ears are depressed and drawn backwards, but not closely to the head; and his lips hang loosely.[4]

Figure 18. Greeting behaviour. Sometimes mistaken for a hostile gesture, sometimes for a sexual advance, this is in fact a purely friendly gesture. It's not so friendly to people if the dog's paws are muddy. From *The Expression of the Emotions in Man and Animals* by Charles Darwin.

It seems odd to me that Darwin does not actually describe the dog rising up on hind legs, putting his forepaws on the object of his affections. He does, however, refer to the figure above that shows this position. Darwin's caption reads, "The same [dog previously shown with hostile intent] caressing his master." The contortion of the dog's body in the illustration surprised me because Crispin keeps his back ramrod straight at this time.

As I noted before, there are those who attribute this behaviour entirely to obeisance owed to an alpha. In the military service one is required to salute a superior officer. That it is required does not mean there cannot be genuine respect, admiration, even liking for the person saluted. The fact that instinct teaches the dog how to show respect for the leader does not rule out the possibility that he genuinely feels that respect, even love.

Dog owners often discourage this behaviour but dog lovers who are not owners tend to like it.

I happen to know that later on, you're going to mention that one of the reasons why humans think people welcomed wolves into their camps was that the wolves would protect the turf they both lived on. So why get so upset if I do the same thing? And why get upset if I give people a warm greeting?

I almost forgot. Crispin does not shed. We have to get him groomed two or three times a year, but what a boon it is to avoid hair discarded all over the house and our clothes. This comes from being a Schnauzer-Wheaten Terrier, two non-shedders. It makes up for a lot of trouble. Also, as his fur gets longer, he looks more and more like a Gund doll, as a friend once insisted he really must be. On the other hand, a non-shedding dog has to have hair cuts, which means taking him to the groomer three or four times a year. It's not a job for amateurs to cut a squirming dog's hair uniformly all over. Not cheap either.

I don't know what shedding means but this grooming is no fun. In fact, it's rather demeaning to be bathed, dried with one of those noisy machines that make a wind, and then be held down while someone cuts off your hair.

Figure 19. The doll that looks like Crispin. We do not know who the manufacturer was but it resembles the enchanting Gund dolls.

11 Out in the World

WE NEED TO REVIEW what the outside is like for Crispin. Recall that he started life in a quiet farm-like atmosphere, then moved to downtown Toronto, a very large, noisy city. After he completed two years there we moved to Victoria, a small city by comparison with Toronto. Of interest to dogs and their owners, there are many beaches in and near our new city, great places for dogs to run and play. When we first moved here, we lived in a single house, with a nice back yard in which we could allow Crispin to run or wander unattended. Four years later we downsized, moving to a smaller, attached town house with correspondingly smaller yard, but Crispin can still have unattended access to it. No room to run, but still possible to dig and harass birds and occasional squirrels.

We have a bird feeder in the yard regularly visited mainly by various breeds of small birds, mainly sparrows and chickadees. Occasionally, we see a Cooper's Hawk whose speciality is raiding bird feeders used by small birds. The target is the birds, not the seeds. I would love to see Crispin chase this guy away or otherwise dispose of him, thereby putting some of his turf protection to good use.

* * *

Most outside time is spent walking. A walk has to start with preparations: getting the leash, making sure there is a supply of plastic bags for collections, a few small biscuits, and depending on time of day and weather, making sure there is a flashlight available and Crispin's coat. Sometimes, if he is sleeping in the living room, one of the humans putting on a coat is sufficient warning that we are going out and he moves toward the door. On the other hand, if the first notice he gets is one of us with the leash in hand, he is likely to try to escape, but our house is small and the attempts are fruitless. It's odd; going out the front door always means the leash, but if he doesn't see it first, he heads for the door when one of us puts on a coat. If he does see the leash first, he plays the catch-me-if-you-can game.

Crispin sometimes sits at the back door, and if no one comes, will give a short bark. I have never heard him similarly bark at the front door, which means going for a walk. Given his elimination habits, it's quite surprising.

Putting on a leash is normally quick and easy. A spring hook attaches to a ring on his collar and that's that. But we use the gentle lead which goes around his snout and that is where his passive resistance begins.

If we are driving somewhere, including to beach areas not close to the house, we walk into the garage, Crispin hops into the car, and off we go. At the waterfront off-leash park we take off his leash and he runs into the grassy areas near where we parked. The humans then usually walk along a path atop a cliff overlooking the Juan de Fuca Strait and Washington State's Olympic Mountains. Crispin follows us, with diversions to explore high grass, woods, bushes and, especially, the many other dogs to be found. He always enjoys being there.

In Toronto it snows a lot. Most dogs like it. They romp around in it like small children, often pushing their snouts into it, then lifting up and tossing the snow about. See a wonderful example of this in a web site, hoping it's still available when you read this.[1] The cold does not bother Crispin. This was proven again when, in December 2008 we had a long spell of snow and sub-zero temperatures. He loved going out in all that. What does bother him and others is getting snow caught between their toes. That's very cold and painful and he seems unable to get rid of it by himself. One way to prevent the problem is to put bootees on him, but he hates them and usually would have them off even before he got outside. In Victoria, we don't have the problem. In our six years here it has only snowed enough to cause a problem three times, but it's never as cold as in Toronto so the snow is usually gone in a day or two.

Why drive when we are within walking distance of the park? Because the nearest entry to the beach area has a point of land extending out into the Strait. This point, like most of this beach, has a steep cliff going down to the water's edge, largely covered with boulders, and leading to the narrow sandy beach. There is a path down the cliff and at the beach there are large rocks, large pieces of driftwood, and tide pools, all wonderful things for dogs or children to explore. Some of the rocks are dangerous for humans to climb on, but not for sure-footed dogs. But the big problem is that Crispin loves it so much that he makes it very difficult to get him back up the hill to begin the trip home.

The dog park in Victoria that we use is about three km long and about 100 meters wide. There are small wooded areas which Crispin loves to explore. It is difficult for a full-grown human to follow him through the low-growing tree branches and bushes. So, we may lose him and it is almost pointless to call him to come because he loves this freedom so much. What I have learned to do is wait at the point we were last together and he will return to it, eventually. So far, "eventually" has never been more than fifteen minutes.

🐕 🐕 🐕

For a walk in the neighbourhood we go outside, down the stairs, up the driveway to the sidewalk. Pause. Which way to go? We can go left which leads to the end of the street and another decision point. Left again takes us to the opposite end of the park that has the off-leash area. This end is a pleasant place to walk, for human or dog. A right turn heads toward downtown, walking on concrete, and looking at store windows. If we had gone to the right at the head of our driveway, we could go right again, toward a small shopping area with lots of people, many with dogs, and the likelihood of meeting a neighbour. Or, we could go straight ahead toward Government House, home of the Lieutenant Governor of the Province.* The House has beautiful gardens and a magnificent view of the Olympic Mountains. Dogs are freely allowed, on leash.

When we first moved into our current house, Crispin always wanted to turn right from the driveway. Left was a better walk, more

* For American readers, a Canadian Lieutenant Governor is the Queen's rerpresentative in a province and is something like a U.S. state governor, but appointed, not elected. Today, the office is mostly ceremonial but the Lt. Governor has some authority to dissolve Parliament or decide which party shall form the government after an electikon. Tradition limits the exercise of these powers.

grass, fewer people. Now, he's used to either. At the end of the block, however, there are further decisions to be made, as just outlined. He does not like new directions. Crispin is a conservative. If right was the way to go yesterday, then right is the way to go today. A week of right turns and it's fixed in his mind. He has occasionally sat down in such a situation and refused to move. You might think it's easy to get a mere eleven kilogram dog up and moving. Not so. I wanted a dog with a mind of his own and I got one. Eventually though, I always win these battles. He can't understand how boring it is for me to go on the same route, look at the same sights, up to three times a day, day after day. For him it is not the same; the smells are ever changing. As we get going, I may try to take a new route. He will resist but not forever.

An interesting aspect of the walk is the commentary we get from passers by. There are the usual comments on what a nice dog he his, but the most frequent question we get is, "Who's walking whom?" It always surprises me how many people seem to think this is an original question. But, it seems to recognize that the dog might well be in charge, and there are times and dogs when this is not so far fetched. The most pleasant form of comment is just the smile that so often appears on the face of the passer-by. They may not say anything, but I can see the eyes are on Crispin and there is a broad smile. It makes me feel good, too.

Yeah, and you can't understand how important it is for a dog to be in familiar territory, among familiar things, smells, dogs and people. The park is nice and so is Government House but it's a long walk to get there and there are few dogs to meet.

There are several things Crispin likes about walking. Number one in his priority is sniffing. I mentioned his typical posture while on a leashed walk, head down, looking like a walking metal detector. He likes to walk on grass but he can be attracted to the smells of a bit of bare concrete as well. He likes to sniff at plants. His favorites are cedar trees, which are common here, often used as hedges, and juniper, both of which are quite fragrant. He likes garden patches but seems to concentrate on the green parts, rather than the blossoms. It's also true that dogs have limited colour perception, so the bright colours of flowers may mean nothing to him. As do most dogs, he likes any surfaces that can be reached and marked in the a dog's own urinary fashion. They like to sniff vertical surfaces to see who's been around lately, also known as checking the p-mail. This goes for tree trunks, fence posts, or the bottom of a building wall.

In this part of the world ocean water is always cold, occasionally quite rough, and only rarely completely calm. We can walk on the beach and Crispin likes to do it. After a winter storm drift wood may be cast up on shore, sometimes entire tree trunks which are fun to

Figure 20. Left: On the search. This is Crispin's usual posture when walking. What is he looking for? Probably tracks of other animals or life's ultimate gift, food. Right: he's found something that needs closer inspection. Photos by C. Meadow.

climb on. On warm days he will wade into the water, but he does not like waves and only on the hottest days will he walk into water above his knees. Once only, I saw him go in until it touched his belly.

Twice when he was a young puppy and we lived on the shore of Lake Ontario, I carried him into the water and gently set him down in it. Both times he swam directly back to shore. The so-called doggie paddle stroke seems nothing more than the dog trying to walk on the water. It works. But neither time was he willing go back in. I gave up.

A few years ago when I temporarily found it physically difficult to go on a vigorous walk with Crispin. He needed the exercise, so we contracted with a company that would pick up the client dogs, take them as a group to some off-leash place, and let them play together for an hour or two. Just dogs. When the need for this passed, it seemed a good idea to continue to let him be with other dogs now and then. It is interesting to watch him join the other dogs, all loaded into a truck or car. They know each other and there is no resentment over another joining the early passengers. This has been a good idea.

> Yes, the beach is a good place to go. I don't understand why you pack leaders get so bothered if I wander away or want to stay longer than you do. I am not interested in running away from home, just to spend more time out in the wild. So, I don't like to swim. I never see you, the alpha member of our pack, going into the water, either.

He's right about that last point.

He loves to roll around in grass. As a man once called out to me from an apartment house balcony from which he saw Crispin rolling on his lawn, "He's a smart dog," clearly meaning he knows where the good grass is. He recognizes well tended lawns, green even in dry weather; even better if newly mowed. (I, too, love the smell of freshly cut grass.) Only recently we discovered Crispin's love of tall grass. He likes to walk through it, perhaps recalling distant ancestors' treks through woods or unmown fields. He also likes to lie down and roll in it.

🐕 🐕 🐕

He still has a great faculty for finding food along the way and is very good, but not perfect, at hiding it from whoever is leading him. The food he finds on and near city streets always amazes me. A typical morsel is a bit of bread or a bone, probably a piece of the thigh bone of a chicken or turkey, or a bit of spare rib or lamb chop but it could be almost as big as a baseball. Sometimes these have clearly been cut by a butcher or some human with a heavy, sharp knife. Where do they come from? Do dogs get them at home and lose them on the street? Do people walk around eating and simply discard the bones? That was obviously the case in downtown Toronto, with lots of fast food places, but seems more unlikely in the prim residential areas of Victoria . Yet, it happens. If he finds a big bone, he picks it up, hides it from me and refuses even a treat while holding it. He does this because, with a big bone, he has to spend time working on it and he seems to know he cannot hide this much activity on the walk. We may get all the way home before he drops it on the floor, ready to attack it again. But that's it. I snatch it away.

Is it an old wives' tale about the danger of chicken bones? No. One time, he suddenly sat down on the sidewalk, quite agitated, and seemed to try to get a paw into his mouth. I thought at first he might have been bitten by some bug or had picked up a fragment of glass in his paw, but then he switched hands, so he wasn't licking a wound. He was trying to reach something. For a few minutes I thought I had never seen an animal in such distress. I tried to open his mouth and look inside, but he did not want me to. Finally, he either loosened the thing with his paw or coughed it up. It was a bone, chicken or turkey, with one end broken and very ragged and sharp. I picked him up, found a nearby spot where I could sit down, and just cradled him for a while. After a few minutes rest he was fine; it was as if nothing happened. Did the experience cure him of picking up stray bones? Of course not. I never found out what the bone did to him — cut his mouth or throat or stick in his throat.

He eats grass now and then, with the inevitable result that he vomits it up later. At the beach in some areas, he may find carcasses of crabs and, now and then, a dead seal. The latter we can see and steer him away from. Oops, that last sentence was written before I recently caught him gnawing at a dead seal, which he got to before I could see what it was and stop him. No harm done but he stank for days. The crab remains can be found and put into his mouth before we can do much. The birds rarely will have left much in the way of meat on the crab, but the aroma is still there. What else may be present are the little organisms that cause disease. There is no way to know how long those remains, of crabs, discarded bones, or even a piece of bread have been festering on the beach.

Another danger, even on a city walk, is a weed commonly called spear grass, although there are several plants that go by this name. One such is shown in figure 21, page 92. This is actually Mediterranean barley, which looks like ordinary grass but has a number of *spikes*. Each of these contains a bundle of *spikelets*, each of which, in turn, contains a seed. A number of long hair-like parts, called *awns*, extend up from the spikelet and shorter growths are on the surface of the spikelet, giving it the rough appearance visible in the figure. As the plant turns brown during in late summer, these various parts be

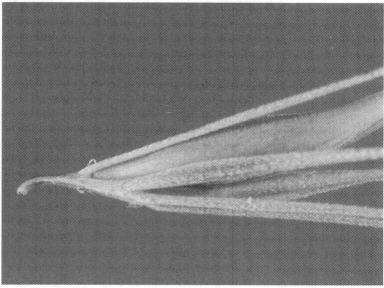

Figure 21. The dreaded spear grass, Mediterranean barley variety. The upper figure shows one spike of the plant containing many spikelets, the thickenings next to the stem. These in turn contain the seeds, one to each spikelet. A seed of this plant is smaller than a grain of rice but larger than a grass seed. The lower picture shows an enlargement of the bottom part of a spikelet. The hook on the end connects it to the stem. That causes a good bit of trouble when embedded in a dog's foot. Upper photo by C. Meadow. Lower one courtesy of the U.S. Department of Agriculture, Jose Hernandez © USDA-NRCS-PLANTS Database.

come stiff. The rough surface of the spikelet then easily attaches the pikelet to a dog's fur. At the end, where the spikelet was attached to the spike, is a barb. Just stepping on the plant can drive that barb, or a sharp awn at the other end, into a dog's foot, requiring surgery to remove it. Another possibility, fortunately less common, is to get a spear into the ear canal. This does not require surgery but does require a general anesthetic because neither dog nor human is likely to tolerate an instrument stuck far into that canal. Crispin has had both procedures.[2]

🐾 🐾 🐾

Crispin is a Terrier and Terriers hunt. Unlike Retrievers, they are the hunters, not just gofers for what someone else has dispatched. He would love to catch a cat but has never been really close to one. Usually the cat sees to that. He also has a hankering for birds. We live among a great many crows and sea gulls. He loves to chase them when they're on the ground, whether because he sees them as food or just for fun, I do not know. I keep telling him he'll never catch one till he learns to fly, but this does not sink in at all.

If it's food, if it's there, I at least try to eat it. Try eating kibble twice a day, day in and day out, and maybe you'd do the same.

🐾

Meeting people and dogs comes next on the priority list. Crispin has not always been especially eager to meet new people but likes to watch and listen to them. He will go up to a small group who are standing and talking on the sidewalk, sit down, look up at them, and act for all the world as if he were part of the conversation. He may do something similar if he comes upon someone working outside. He

once saw a carpenter making a new front stairway for a house, working with a table saw on the lawn. Crispin walked near him, sat down,
and watched the man as intently as the most avid student might. The
man was enchanted. Crispin seems to like to watch any slow motion
and listen to interesting sounds, but not ones that are too loud. He
also goes for games, soccer and softball being what he is most likely to
see, and occasionally cricket here in Victoria. Sometimes when he
stares at a person, I get embarrassed because I wonder if people feel
odd having a dog watching them so intently, almost as if he knew
what they were doing or saying. Regardless of what he does, he still
attracts more than his fair share of admirers as we walk along. It can
be as little as a smile, a stop and talk with me, or petting him.

🐾 🐾 🐾

We once worked with a professional trainer, trying to improve
Crispin's attention to orders. The trainer did a good job and added, in
his assessment, that Crispin was hyper-vigilant; a very apt observation. Whenever there are people or animals around whom he doesn't
know, he must stop and observe, sometimes looking like a pointer
dog. He will stand still, at attention, head pointed toward, and eyes
intently focused on, the object of interest. This can be as normal-
appearing to us as a car coming to a stop along the curb and a person
getting out. Watching people load or unload the car is a bonus for
him. I don't think I have ever seen the person observed this way be
oblivious to it. I can't help assuming that what goes through the person's mind is, "Why is that dog looking at me?" And possibly, "Is he
going to attack?" or "Is this an excuse for the man with him to watch
me?"

During the past year, I have been seeing him initiate a slow approach to a stranger, move closer, and welcome the proffered hand for

a sniff. Does he recognize some quality of the person? He clearly pre-
fers women. Dogs are believed to be able to tell the difference,
whether among dogs or people. Those to whom he deigns to give
such attention always like him, but who wouldn't like being singled
out by a cute dog? There are dog phobic people who don't seem to be
on his approach list. Much as I like to attribute this behaviour to
friendliness, I wonder if he isn't attracted by some food-related smell.

🐕 🐕 🐕

If Crispin meets a dog on the walk anything can happen; the
range of reactions goes from immediate liking to immediate hostility.
Immediate liking typically means a rapid move toward the other dog
and an offer to play. He doesn't do much actual playing any more but,
with the right dog, the memory of puppy-like behaviour is recalled.
The opposite extreme is reserved for certain breeds, such as bulldogs,
all of whom he particularly dislikes, for reasons unknown. In between
the extremes are passive tolerance of the other dog's offer to play,
complete disinterest, and a minimal aggressive act of lowering his
head and growling. Actual combat – never unless initiated by the
other dog.

Most owners will ask about the other dog's friendliness or assert
whether theirs is friendly or not. In the latter case there is a warning
to keep away. So much for the other guy. Crispin's radar tells him that
some dogs mean trouble and he approaches them slowly and deliberately with head down and muscles tight, a sign of fear or potential
aggression, or both. Then, I kneel down and talk soothingly to him,
saying what a nice dog this is coming toward us. Crispin, of course,
does not understand this, but I feel my tone of voice calms him. Not
always. Sometimes, the two dogs approach each other, do a prelimi-
nary nose to nose sniff, and immediately snap at each other. Typically,

this happens so fast the two owners cannot even tell who started it or why. This is why leashes are a good idea; the dogs can be quickly separated. The bulldog case is like this. Some of them are quite friendly. I have never known one to act hostile before Crispin did, but there it is, a predictable reaction.

Recently, Crispin and I went to a training program aimed at solving or alleviating these meeting problems. Perhaps the key thing I learned is that a dog senses the mood of the person leading him, as well as of the other dog and the other dog's leader. If the leader is nervous and tightens up on the leash, the dog feels this and may decide to protect the leader from what he or she seems to have decided is a threat. Most of the time, of course, it is not a threat, it's human worry that causes the dog to worry. We also learned that the sure way to avoid trouble is to steer clear of the other dog before trouble happens.

> Once again, I think you don't understand. Dogs have to protect their territory and their pack and have to be prepared to fight if necessary. I guess you humans don't have that problem or else you don't do the job well. The way to avoid a fight is to get the other dog to see that it would not be in his best interests to start one.

I find that I think in terms of two kinds of walks – his and mine. If it's his, that means it is one of the usually three daily walks for his exercise and relief. I am very tolerant of his dawdling and sniffing. Walking a single block can easily take ten minutes. The other walk is mine – we are going someplace specific and I don't want much of that dawdling. He takes this in stride, but needs frequent reminding.

Here's something unexpected to me. He has spent at least one night in, or has visited often in, several houses in Victoria. When he walks by such a house now, he turns into the walk leading to the front door. It has been about six years since he stayed in the first house and the memory seems to be fading. He still stops in front of this one, but seems uncertain, does not go onto the walk toward the door, but sits down, pondering. He did the same in another case where the people moved away three years ago. All the others still attract him and he moves directly as if to go in.

> Knowing where you live is important to any dog and knowing where a previous den had been established was needed for survival by my wolf ancestors.

I started taking him for walks in Toronto where we would walk the city streets at night. It was rather quiet after 10 PM in our neighbourhood. I always found the walks rather relaxing for me and, of course, necessary for him. I still feel that way. Walking with Crispin is not uproarious fun but is a very pleasant experience.

There are other things a dog might do outside: just run around, chase squirrels, cats, and birds, explore woods and rocky areas. Being a Terrier, he early showed a drive to chase small animals, other than dogs. As mentioned earlier he once caught a rat, but did not kill it. He has never caught any others and is gradually losing interest in the chase.

I don't know where his liking for rocky areas comes from, but it was apparent as soon as we moved to Victoria where there are rocky beaches and outcrops of rock all over. He likes to climb high and then survey his domain. The advantage of being small and four-footed becomes apparent in rock climbing. If he trips or slips, he does not have far to fall and his center of gravity is always between his four legs, so he is much harder to topple over than a human is.

In running, Crispin is not particularly fast compared with most other dogs, but he does enjoy it. If he meets another dog of his liking, off-leash, one of them might start running and the other will chase. Nothing happens when the chaser catches up. They both may stop, rest a moment, then resume running.

Like race horses, dogs have different gaits depending on the speed they want and endurance they will need.[3] These are illustrated in figures 22 and 23. At walking speed, shown in figure 22a, the left front- and right hind legs are in step as are the other two legs. If the dog wants to increase speed, still in moderation, he switches to a trot (figure 22b). This is similar to the walking gait, but his stride is longer and speed is greater. Finally, if he is really in a hurry he gallops like a horse (figure 22c). That means the hind legs now work together as do the forelegs. The two hind legs push; essentially, the animal is jumping forward. The forelegs hit the ground first and pull the body forward a little. There are moments when all four feet are off the ground, also true of speeding horses. This phenomenon is best illustrated in figure 23 where the light-coloured dog has all feet off the ground, while the darker one in the foreground seems to have only his left fore-leg on the ground. A fraction of a second earlier, that leg would have been off the ground, too.

Time out now for reminiscing. I was in England one spring at lambing time. I was riding on a train on a beautiful day and passed a field, very green and full of new-born lambs. They looked like cotton balls with feet. They were all running about, uncoordinated, just running and tumbling. I have hardly ever heard the word *gamboling* used in any other context. It just made me laugh, not at them, but with them. The scene was the perfect representation of the word joy. What

Figure22a. Walking gait for dogs.

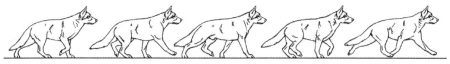

Figure 22b. Trotting gait for dogs.

Figure 22c. A horse galloping. This is quite a different gait from trotting. Dogs use a similar gait when running at full speed. These three figures are by courtesy of and copyright by Linda Shaw.

Figure 23. Galloping gait used by racing Greyhounds. Photo pourtesy of Darold Robertson, Able Acres Farm.

has this to do with Crispin? He has a way of running, a sort of slow gallop, using the gallop gait but going much slower. He typically does this when he sees, at a distance, a dog or person he thinks he will like and runs toward him or her. Every time I see it I am reminded of those lambs and a big smile comes across my face.

> We depend on smells to mark a trail and can make noise as a signal and get a sound signal back. If we go out hunting but can't find our way home, we're in serious trouble.
> As for the various strides, an animal who lives outside may have to go a long way to find food and run fast to get it or get away from an enemy. We learn how to conserve energy when we can and run at top speed when we have to.

12 Traveling

WE HAVE TRAVELED quite a bit since Crispin joined the family. Traveling without him means finding someone to take care of him. The first time we did this, we left him in a kennel near Toronto, which was clean and neat, well organized, very professional. Dogs left there were not going to catch diseases from other dogs because they never had direct contact with other dogs. Comforting at first to the owners, but not much fun for the dog. Eventually, we came to realize that while fun may not be the main objective, the objective should be to put the dog in an environment where he will feel secure and comfortable. Socializing with other dogs is a way to achieve this and perhaps to reduce the sense of abandonment on the dog's part. The next place we found to leave him was in a private home with a family who had a dog of their own and boarded others, fed them and walked them. OK, not sterile, but more comforting for him and us. There is an immunization for a disease known informally as kennel cough and formally as bordatella and a half dozen other, less formal, names. Crispin has had this shot so we don't worry about it if we leave him where dogs are in close contact with each other.

In Victoria our first success with boarding was with a neighbouring family whose children wanted a dog of their own, so the parents thought that boarding dogs for a while would serve as a test experience. It went well for both families. They liked Crispin and he liked them. They did get their own dog and the two get along well, although they do not see each other often.

We also had some friends who were happy to have him at their house for a few days at a time. He was quite happy with them. When they moved into an apartment that banned dogs, we had to look farther afield. Other friends knew him well and had a house on two unfenced acres in which he was free to run around. One member of the household, Steven, was recovering from surgery one time when we needed to travel. He had to stay home and do nothing more strenuous than look out for Crispin; a perfect fit. An odd thing about any of Crispin's visits to this house is that he has never gone exploring through the whole two acres. He always stays within sight of the house.

When Steven recovered and wanted to get back to his work as an artist, we found another instance of a person taking dogs into her own house as boarders. This is a business for her, so more facilities are available and more room for the dogs, both inside and outside than in most homes used for boarding. Hers has a good size yard to run free in and lots of company of other dogs, so we're now content on this front.

Yet another possibility is our daughter, Debra, who lives in Portland, Oregon. It is not convenient to go there if we are traveling east or north, but if we are going south, it's great. She and her partner, Paul, have a house with a friendly dog named Tucker, a Norwegian

Figure 24. Tucker. Here is a dog who barks rather fiercely if any strangers approach the house, but that ends the hostility. He is actually very friendly. He and Crispin get along well, Crispin understands that Tucker belongs to the house, so to speak, and accepts his dominance. Photo by C. Meadow.

Elk Hound (at least partly). Crispin, as most dogs would, accepts Tucker, who's bigger than him, as the boss and they get along well and are well looked after.

> Yes, I like going to Deb and Paul's house and I like Tucker. He doesn't play much but he likes to run about and doesn't bother me if I don't feel like following him. He barks when someone comes to the door, like I do, but then he is quiet and accepts the new person.

The next question is how to travel with Crispin. I'm sure all readers have seen dogs happily sticking their heads out of a car window and enjoying the breeze and the views. Not our guy. As a puppy he was subject to motion sickness, a condition I am sure he inherited from me. He has gradually outgrown that, but his typical stance when in the car is either lying down sleeping, or sitting up with his head against the back of the seat. Sometimes, if he is in the back seat, he moves forward, with his feet on the little storage box between the two front seats and either looks through the windshield or just seems to enjoy being up with the people. Sudden braking spoils that pose.

On a long trip we have to find hotels or motels that accept pets. Many do, many don't. Those that do tend to charge an extra fee, from $10-20 a night up and may ask for a deposit of $50, promptly returned if all goes well. We have found it to be truly prompt. Lately, they have insisted that the pet may never be left alone in the room. Actually, that's sensible, because if a staff member goes into a room to clean, deliver towels, or whatever, a dog could really make trouble. Even if locked in his crate could raise a great fuss and frighten the person. So, we leave Crispin in the car when we go out to eat on the road, and he is reasonably content with this.

The second requirement for traveling with pooch is finding places for him to exercise and relieve himself. This is not always easy. In Santa Rosa, California we found an off-leash park near the hotel, quite nice and much appreciated. At other times we have to settle for a small stretch of grass such as a border around a gas station. Washington State has some nice rest stops on Interstate Highway 5 where dogs can be walked on grass. Of course, whether we find something nice or not, it is necessary to stop at least three times daily. This cuts into a long day of making good mileage, but is a relief to our arthritic backs and knees.

We always bring water, a water dish and a supply of his food to last the entire trip. That way, he does not have to adapt to any new food. Once, however, on entry into the U.S., the customs officer saw Crispin and asked if we had dog food with us. We did, of course, and he asked to see it. It contained beef, among other things, and was made in Canada. We found that this beef was not permitted to enter the United States – some hangover from the mad cow disease scare. So, the officer confiscated it. As a result, we shifted to a new brand that consisted mainly of lamb and rice and was made in the U.S.A. No more customs problems. And it costs less.

🐕 🐕 🐕

Sometimes we all have new experiences together. In California there is a redwood tree with what amounts to a tunnel cut through it into which cars can drive. I had seen a picture of this when I was in the fourth grade in school and always wished to see such a magic tree. The figure on p. 106 shows our car, Mary Louise driving, and Crispin advising, as they passed through the tunnel.

Some dogs like to stick their fool heads out of a car window, or chase sticks into cold water, or get carried everywhere in a stupid bag slung around the owner's neck. Dogs were not made to look out of car windows. And yes, I used to get sick in the car and still feel a bit queasy sometimes. Sleep is the best way to avoid this. Riding in a car all day, even with three walks, is hardly exciting.

Sometimes, I have to admit, we all get in the car and when we get out we're at some new and interesting place that's fun to explore.

🐾

Figure 25. Crispin in the redwood tree. On a trip to California we wtook this opportunity to drive our car through an opening carved out of this enormous tree. Photo by C. Meadow.

13 The Down Side

I HOPE I have made enough points about the upside of keeping a dog. But, just as with raising children, however much we love them, there is another side. Dogs make great time demands of their owners; their medical care must be paid for, and so must their food, although food for a small dog is a minor issue. There are times when it is necessary to get someone else to take care of them, say when the owners are away. There are certain places the owners like or would like to go to from which dogs are barred. And, finally, perhaps not so much on the farm, but in the city, they must be walked, fed, cleaned, and pampered. Finally, I am sure that most dogs, sooner or later misbehave in ways that vary from embarrassing to expensive.

🐾 🐾 🐾

The most obvious time demands are when the dog has to go for a walk, to the vet, to the groomer, or to his bath, just as with children. Also as with children, you cannot leave a young dog alone for too long. What constitutes too long has to be determined by experiment. You do not leave either child or dog alone in a locked car with the windows up, on a hot day. You should not leave a puppy alone with your antique furniture even for ten minutes. At least there are no soccer or piano lessons for the dog, but there is obedience school. Is this situation bad? No, it just is. You have a choice: (a) spend the time, (b) don't have a dog, or (c) don't spend the time and have a neurotic dog. Less obvious and not really requiring much time, but interrupting other things, is getting up to let him in or out, and waking up to calm him when the crows and sea gulls start their 5:30 AM serenade. If you really like the dog, most of these demands on you are not really bad, in fact much is pleasurable, but life is not the same as before.

🐕 🐕 🐕

The medical costs for a dog can be more than for a child if you have decent family health insurance. Dog insurance helps but is expensive. Crispin was still in his first year when he contracted what was tentatively diagnosed as acute pancreatitis. Oh, was he sick. Blood came out both ends. He paid no attention to anything or anyone around him. Off we went to the veterinary emergency hospital. The next day he was somewhat better and was referred back to his own vet for another night. The hospital bill was for $1100. The bill for the next night in the local lock-up was $300+. From that he emerged a tired version of his old self, but was soon fully right again. I had four children and never paid a medical bill that large. We applied for and got pet medical insurance. The original price in 2003 was about $40 per month. Now, it's over $50, or $600+ per year and there is a stiff deductible amount. By comparison, we pay $1300 per year for our government health insurance that covers doctor and hospital visits for Mary Louise and me and we pay about $1000 a year for extended health care for ourselves that pays most pharmacy and dental bills and out-of-country medical charges. An annual visit to the vet is about $100 and rabies or other shots are extra. Visits for small illnesses or injuries cost about $50. A visit to the emergency hospital costs more, but you go because there seems to be some urgency or need for more surgery than can be done in the vet GP's office and, of course, the really bad things always happen when the office is closed.

Grooming sessions cost about $50 each, but only three or four times a year. His food is inexpensive. An 11-kg dog doesn't eat a great deal.

All told, he's an expensive hobby, perhaps almost as much as playing golf. But far nicer.

🐾 🐾 🐾

While food is not a major issue for us, it could be for some dogs. Crispin eats two-thirds cup or about 160 ml. of kibble per day, in two servings. We usually flavor it with a bit of cheese or egg or small bits of meat or fish. It takes far less time to feed him than it does a human. Some owners are addicted to cakes and biscuits made just for dogs. Yes, there are dog bakeries in many cities. I've never been to one, but I do remember a dog birthday party in Toronto at which all the dogs were treated to a cake from one such establishment. We are not addicted to this. Crispin is overjoyed with the skin from a broiled salmon. Who needs special cakes? Why do we even bring up the cost of food? Even if not major cost, neither is it free.

🐾 🐾 🐾

Care and boarding costs depend on family life style. We have been traveling a lot lately and, although I like to take Crispin with us, it's not always feasible. Airlines have mixed records on shipping pets. Live or healthy arrival is not guaranteed and some airlines will not guarantee shipment of the pet on the flight the owners are taking. I assume that rule is to discourage shipment of animals in any case. Some hotels prefer not to have them as do as some people you might want to visit. Further, taking the dog by car means stopping more than some people like, for exercise and relief stops. But, after all, he's fun to have around.

Boarding at a commercial kennel has typically cost us about $20-25 a night and some excellent ones are available. Short-term care can be provided by professional dog walkers or helpful friends or neighbouring teenagers. We have never used a young neighbour because of the demographics of our neighbourhood, but I have noticed that some youngsters are not patient with their charges. Be careful to be sure your helper really likes animals. I described our professional service in the previous chapter. These people are good at their work and if we stick to the same days and times, Crispin will be with dogs he has come to know and with whom he gets along. Cost is also about $20 for a morning or afternoon, including pick up and delivery and driving them all to a place they enjoy.

🐾 🐾 🐾

When we lived in Toronto we found that dogs were permitted on busses, street cars, and subways. The same was true in England when we lived there for a year. In eighteen years of living in Toronto I never even heard of a problem caused by this policy. When we moved to Victoria, a veddy British place although the ethnicity is being diluted by immigrants, such as we, we were surprised to find that there are relatively few apartment houses, whether rental or condominium, that will allow a dog. They are allowed on busses only if in a box or cage. They are permitted in most parks only on leash. In spite of all this it sometimes seems that half the population has a dog. All the rest must have cats, since they abound and have no restrictions on their wanderings. Some of our citizenry want to restrict cat wanderings because they sometimes kill birds. That would mean converting all outside cats to indoor cats, not likely to please the outdoor cats. One might as well say that a solution to bird droppings on your patio is to deny birds the right to fly.

So, we live in a dog infested city that is not always hospitable to dogs, but there are enough of us owners to keep going.

🐾 🐾 🐾

One of the costs of dog ownership is misbehaviour. The most common form is completely natural – chewing. This is a puppy phenomenon. As the dog grows up, the problem normally disappears. With children aged almost one to perhaps four or five, it is possible to childproof the house. This means mostly moving breakable or dangerous objects out of reach. It isn't that easy with dogs because they are quite happy to chew on the legs of your antique table and they can jump onto tables. We were once visiting a cousin who deals in oriental carpets. Just in time he managed to stop Crispin from peeing on one of his prize holdings. We assumed it was an animal smell that came with the rug that attracted the attention and needed his mark recorded on top.

Another problem is that some people simply don't like dogs or are afraid of them. Some of these may be your best friends. For Crispin and many other dogs, their way of showing friendship is to touch the friend. For example, such a phobic friend and I were out walking one day when the friendly and uninhibited Golden Retriever, belonging to a neighbour, came up to my friend, stood up and placed his paws on the friend's shoulders. For a moment, I was sure cardiac arrest was imminent. The friend froze, the right thing to do, and the dog simply walked away. I was sorry for the friend, liked the dog and his owners, and could think of no way to stop any other dog from doing the same thing. Seems to me that everyone should be a dog lover, but in truth they are not all that lovable.

There are worse things yet a dog can do or cause. It's a long enough saga to deserve a chapter of its own, coming up next.

Ooh, I didn't know about most of this. I don't know what money is, but it seems important to Alpha. Sorry if I've been too much of a burden. Dogs don't have money in their own societies. Is it a good idea?

14 Threats and Security

CRISPIN AT ONE TIME acted as the family security officer. As reported earlier, he would bark at strangers coming near our front door and, when on leash, at other dogs coming near him that he did not know. He gradually gave up most of this behaviour. The problems, I believe, were mostly caused by fear, either on his own behalf or the family's. He still reacts loudly at the door bell and many people tell us that's good security. Our old friend Shadow apparently never chased away a burglar. We can't know this for sure, of course, but we do know there were several burglaries while he was in the house and he was big enough that a show of force should have chased away most intruders. So, maybe the noise is worth it.

Let's consider some of the kinds of incidents and assumed feelings that have caused at least minor problems in the past.

At the bottom of the list, in terms of the seriousness of the problem, is his feeling that he may be unable to defend himself, or us, if necessary – he feels an attack might be imminent. I've described this in terms of his worry about other dogs when on the leash. The same happens if he is tied up. We never do this in our own yard; we rely on fencing. But on a walk when it is desirable to step into a store for a short time, how easy it is to tie him to some near-by post. I see lots of dogs secured this way and find that, overwhelmingly, they are at peace with the passing world. We used to do this in Toronto and were unaware of any consequences.

Crispin today is not at peace when tied up. In fact, we have since learned it is illegal in Victoria to tie a dog up in a public place. He gets very nervous. I have twice seen him snap at a passer-by who approached him while tied up, but he did no more than that. I have never tied him since seeing these occurrences. Snapping is not the same as biting. It might not even be intended to touch the supposed target. Or, he might intend to, but only to nip him. A nip is not like the infamous bite of a Pit Bull. Its purpose is clearly to send a message, not defeat an enemy. Human parents do such things when they swat the rear end of a child fortified by a diaper. It is not intended to cause pain but to send a message. All this does not prevent some people from becoming frightened or outraged at a nip or a snap. On the other hand, the very ambiguity of the situation can justify fear on the part of someone who is not familiar with dogs, and even some who are familiar. Caution is always in order when meeting a strange dog.

> I already explained how important it is for a dog to be ready to fight. Being on leash is bad enough. Being tied up but allowing strangers to come near me is too much.

The next level is when the dog feels he is under attack. Unfortunately, this can happen with a small child who, with only the most benign intent, scares the dog. It might be by wiggling fingers directly in front of his face, as people often do with human babies. I have seen this described as the dog seeing the flashing teeth of another animal. It can even be done by a stranger moving a hand to pat him on the head. Crispin doesn't snap in this case, but he retreats quickly. A girl of about five or six once did this, with the reaction I just described and asked me why he pulled away. I put my hand out and moved it about six inches over her head. She did exactly what Crispin had done. If she had been an adult, I could have said QED, but I pointed out that she didn't like it either and the meaning seemed to get through to her.

When two dogs who do not know each other meet, the result can range from immediate friendship to immediate hostilities. Most owners are baffled by this because it happens so fast and we humans are often unable to see the signs that caused the problem. This seems usually to be based on fear, rather than anything overt.

When an adult human, not previously known, approaches Crispin, he is going to be more cautious than with children. Again, an innocent motion or gesture can seem like a threat or attack even if benignly intended. The dog's response may be more vigorous than with children. We had one case of this; a neighbour who did exercise walking, making swift, determined strides, came past our house. I'm sure no harm was intended, but the dog was not used to the man's motions. Also, he was not used to being outside, in front, unrestrained.

I did not see the encounter, but Crispin nipped the man. I heard about it when our doorbell rang and a strange man began yelling at me that I should keep my dog restrained. To cut the story short, he called the police. A young officer came. Crispin barked when he rang. When the door opened, the officer took one look at him and laughed.

He owned a dog, too, of a much larger breed. I guess he wondered just how much harm Crispin could do. We explained that we never knowingly let him run free and that someone working at our house had left open a gate we never used, so we did not notice it was open. That was how Crispin got out. It turned out the man was only scratched. The officer passed on our apologies and the war was over. Good police work; a battle defused in a few minutes.

> Again, it's a matter of being ready. When the first of those dogs who bit me started to attack, I was on leash, not free to fight or run. The second time, I was off leash but never saw it coming. Both dogs were much bigger than me, so I might not have been able to fight them off even if I did see them and was free. When that man made gestures toward me that I was not familiar with, but I thought were hostile, I took action in defense.

I guess that those gestures Crispin refers to were something intended to shoo him away, but as with the fingers in the face, this could easily be misinterpreted.

When the apparent threat is to a family member or friend, Crispin can get more excited yet. There were two such incidents. One when he was about one year old and one when he was five. In the earlier case we were at a beach. Mary Louise was in the water; I was walking Crispin on leash, on the sand. A woman suddenly arose from the water, between us and Mary Louise. Crispin lunged at the woman and scratched her. She wasn't much bothered but her husband was. Nothing came of it. Our male protected his female; the other woman's male defended her. But it was certainly a matter of concern. How often were we going to see this happen? Or was this just a puppy escapade?

It took four years to happen again. This time we were away. Crispin was staying with his favorite dog walker, Lori. She, Crispin, her boyfriend and his dog were sitting at an outside table at a coffee house. The boyfriend went inside to order. Lori tied Crispin to the table as her friend had with his dog, and went in to join the boyfriend. Another woman came along, following right behind the walker. Crispin had enough slack to jump at her, again inflicting a minor injury. The victim was forgiving. No consequences. What was similar here was that he perceived his female companion to be at risk by this woman and the risk appeared quite suddenly. No reasonable human would have considered either of these situations to be a threat. The message to us is to be careful when he perceives a female of his pack to be threatened, even if only temporarily. Only women? So it seems. Can he tell the difference? Yes.

Crispin is now eight years old, usually much calmer and wiser.

Just recently, though, it happened again. This time two women, known to me but not Crispin or Mary Louise, came to our house and rang the doorbell. There was the usual reaction by Crispin and I, as usual, made him sit down and stop barking before I opened the door. As I turned to open it, Crispin moved in front of me, as did Mary Louise. I assumed that, as usual, he would now greet the visitors in a friendly way. Instead, he now with his alpha female behind him and a stranger in front,charged at the first visitor and bit her on the leg. It happened so fast I didn't even see that he had bitten her, but I knew he had charged at her, making his most aggressive noises. The woman he bit took it calmly. She was a dog owner herself. What happened? In retrospect, it seemed to me to be another case of his feeling the need to protect the female member of our pack, another Don Quixote reaction. And again, it seems that the solution has to be to convince him that Mary Louise can be in charge when strangers are around and can take care of herself and him.

In our world males are normally bigger and stronger than females of the same breed and age. That's why they need protecting. In both the cases you mention, the attacker (the one who seemed to be attacking) did what wolves do — separate the target from the main group, and attack. You seem to assume these people were not planning to attack. Should I have known this? Should I have just sat there and watched?

What if Crispin or Mary Louise is really under attack? I mentioned two other instances before where he was attacked. To review, they came in the second and third month of our residence in Victoria, less than thirty days apart, but in different locations and involving different attackers. Crispin was then two years old. In case one, he and I were walking, he on leash, in the early evening of December 16, my birthday. Suddenly, we both saw another dog, a Black Lab, unattended and unrestrained. I guessed he weighed about 30 kilos, three times Crispin's weight. The two dogs looked at each other for a couple of seconds, then the stranger attacked. It was fast and vicious. Crispin was quickly on the ground, on his back, legs in the air – the dog symbol of surrender. The attacker bit anyway. At that point I was able to chase him away. I thought I recognized him as a neighbour's dog. Another neighbour saw the fracas and called animal control. Because we were new in town, I didn't want to begin our presence by calling the cops on a neighbour. I did call the people who I believed were the owners and asked if the dog had been immunized against rabies. The husband came over to our house, papers in hand, and apologized. The caller, I found out, had a dog who had been bitten by the same attacker and we found this had happened to many other dogs in the neighbourhood. The wife of the owning family insisted to animal control that it could not have been her dog. I knew her only slightly and found her a most pleasant person. The animal control of-ficer felt that biting a dog who was submitting is not normal canine practice, indicating a problem dog, and there had been reports of other incidents. He required the owners to post a dangerous dog sign and gave a warning or hint that he could have had the animal de-stroyed. Not long after, the family that owned the dog moved away. Neighbourhood gossip had it that the dog was later involved in an-other attack on a dog and left town as quickly as possible. I cannot verify this, except for the move.

Shortly after this, in January, in daylight, Mary Louise was walk-ing Crispin off leash in our favorite dog park. Another dog, not clearly identifiable by breed but seemingly with some Rottweiler in him, jumped Crispin and bit him on the back of the neck. It was a deep puncture wound. Biting at that spot is what canines do when really out for a kill. Mary Louise got the name of the owner, called animal control, and the story from the owner of the attacker was that, yes, there had previously been such problems but not lately, and he's a good dog. I do not know if there were consequences for dog or owner. We had high vet bills, fortunately insured.

In both cases, the attacker acted unlike most dogs – an all-out at-tack without warning or apparent cause. In both cases an owner was in denial. Were we in denial about our problems with Crispin?

Two other dog stories illustrate that not all dogs, even of the so-called vicious breeds, are necessarily vicious. Both involve Pit Bulls and I was either involved or a witness to both. In the first case I had taken Crispin to the beach, one of the times I tried to interest him in swimming. I had taken off my shoes to wade in a bit, and was now sitting on the ground putting my shoes back on. This is not a posture in which a person is ready for a fight. I looked up and saw a Pit Bull coming at me at full-speed. Before I could even move he was in my lap, licking my face. Then, he turned around and ran back to his owner, near by. I was astonished. Everyone knows this is not supposed to happen. I should have been mauled. Not long after, in the dog park we frequented in Toronto, there was a young Pit Bull named Travis who was a regular. He was well trained, just a pup, and although he played roughly he never seemed to be mean. There was also a young man in a wheel chair who often came to watch the dogs. He had cerebral palsy or some condition that affected most of his muscles, so that he moved and talked with difficulty but had a charming face. Travis ran over to him. Clearly, an attack was in progress. He put his paws on the man's lap, reached up and licked his face. The man in the chair grinned like the sun shining after a rain. I remember feeling that it was not likely he had many such spontaneous experiences from a stranger, not a kiss meaning "I'm so sorry for you," but meaning "I like you."

So, what to make of these stories? Dogs, like people, should be taken one at a time. Not all Pit Bulls are bad and probably not all Shelties or Golden Retrievers are good, even though they always look it to me.

> Sounds good. Take each dog as an individual. But anyone who doesn't take extra care when a Pit Bull approaches is nuts. There are other breeds that always seems ready and eager to fight, so I must be ready.

The final problem was serious. We were visiting my daughter in Portland. Somehow, no one remembered letting him out, Crispin got out of the house and was exploring the large yard. A neighbour across the street was coming over, bringing a plate of cookies as a gift. As she told it, Crispin attacked her, she fell or was knocked down, ended up in hospital with a broken pelvis. She was quite elderly. She was not used to or knowledgeable about dogs and she was the only witness. We felt it was out of character for him to attack when there was no threat. Further, his normal reaction to someone carrying aromatic things, was to jump up and down, looking for a handout. (He was still quite young.) A dog can do just so much jumping up and down on his hind legs before he needs to support himself momentarily by placing his front paws on the person with the goodies. We felt this is what happened and she got frightened, turned to run, and fell, feeling that Crispin pushed her. What he did, if he did it, may well have felt like a push. Running is useless if a dog is truly attacking. Few of us can outrun one in the short race. Legally, we were at fault. We cannot attribute any part of the woman's subsequent claim to trying to cash in on us. She and her family were on good terms with my daughter's family and her honesty is not in question. Because there were no witnesses, her word was all there was. We, of course, think she was mistaken in what was going on. Indisputably, she was hurt and while our angel was involved, we think it was not actually an attack.

Could Crispin have thought the house he was temporarily living in needed protection from this frail lady? It doesn't fit any of the other patterns we have seen. It looks like bad luck for both of us, and a reminder that dog owners are responsible for what their dogs do. Were we, too, in denial?

We turned the whole thing over to our insurance company, which settled amicably. We then consulted our veterinarian and a professional animal trainer. The vet suggested a few possibilities, including what amounted to tranquilizing drugs and even brought up the ultimate, for which the euphemism is putting down. I was devastated even by the thought, but had to agree that, however much we loved the dog, we could not maintain an animal who might repeatedly do this sort of thing, even if it was all unintentional this time. We found a professional animal trainer who gave some good advice, worked some with Crispin, and did a great deal of good.

> I dint do nuttin' except go for the cookies. How was I to know how that woman would react? As soon as I showed an interest in the cookies, she started to run away and she fell.

❖

Whatever actually happened, it appears that, with increasing age, such incidents are less likely to recur. In his own neighbourhood he is calm and affectionate. Strangers can usually safely enter the house if we let them in. Children can approach and pet him in the street, but we hold him and explain to any parent who seems to need it that it is always a good idea to be cautious when a child and a dog, any child and any dog, come together for the first time. I'm finding that most parents know this and appreciate the precaution and want their children not to be overly afraid of dogs.

I guess we all have to remember that dogs have a lot of wolf left in them, in spite of thousands of years of domestication, and we require them to live in a human world, governed by human rules and morals, which they cannot fully understand.

> I agree with this.

❖

Part III Origin, Communication, Thinking, and Emotion

In this part there is more about dogs in general than Crispin alone. Understanding what dogs are like helps a great deal in understanding any one in particular.

Because we (human owners, observers, scientists) and the dogs do not speak the same language, we may never be sure what a dog understands of what we say or signal. And dogs, of course, have the same difficulty in knowing what we understood of what they are trying to tell us.

15 Where Dogs Come From

I HAVE ALWAYS enjoyed watching Crispin explore his world, but for me to understand that world I need some explanation of what it means to be a Terrier and to see where Terriers came from. While there are disagreements among experts on many aspects of the evolutionary story, it is generally agreed that dogs are descended from wolves who, in evolutionary terms, are a very old race. Specifically, dogs are of the species *Canis familiaris* and the closest wolf ancestor is the grey wolf, *Canis lupus*. *Canis* covers a family of similar animals including dogs, hyenas, coyotes, and dingos, in addition to wolves. Wolves are believed to have originated, or descended from their ancestors in Asia several million years ago. There is no exact number because the appearance of wolves or any species was not an instantaneous occurrence. It happened over a long period of time, although, as we shall see, dogs emerged from wolves over a relatively short period.[1]

To the non-expert, the grey wolf looks much like some breeds of sled dogs, particularly the Alaskan Malamute. Once again, we have no exact date for when *C. lupus* became *C. familiaris*, but figures of about 15,000 years ago are commonly mentioned.[2] Dogs are believed to be the first species of animal to have been domesticated by humans. The usual theory is that gradually, wolves discovered that our primitive human ancestors had the habit of throwing food scraps away. These were something the wolves were quite happy to eat. As a result, they began to come near the camp sites of these early people. Such a food source was valuable. This garbage pit needed protection from other animals, which could include unfriendly roaming humans. Our ancestors were primitive, but not entirely dumb. They had found

Figure 26. A grey wolf *(Canis lupus)* on the left and a Malamute *(Canis familiaris)* on the right. The Malamute is a dog but looks a great deal like his ancestor. My only experience with one of these dogs was that she was a lovely, gentle creature. I never met the other guy. Wolf photo ©iStockphoto.com/sykadelx. Dog photo © iStock- photo. com/GlobalP.

a defense against predators at no cost. Some wolves even made friends, came into the camp and, by gosh, they were kind of cute. And they might even snuggle up on a cold night, with all that nice thick fur.

🐾 🐾 🐾

No one knows for sure, but some believe that it was the wolves who initiated the transformation to dogs by self-selection of those who became close to the humans. It is also likely that the humans chose to encourage the friendly ones to stay around. There is not a great deal of difference between these theories. The fossil record supports the assumption that the evolution of a species we call dog was quick in evolutionary terms. A modern-day experiment in Siberia took a group of Silver Fox pups, put them in separate cages and treated them well. As the keepers went from cage to cage, feeding or just greeting the pups, they noted which ones seemed less afraid and more friendly toward people. The friendliest ones were mated with each other, and the process repeated. After ten generations, which could have taken not much more than ten years, ten percent of the pups were considered "elite," in terms of their tame behaviour. After 40 generations, and about as many years, the proportion of elites went to 35 percent. A tame species evolved, very dog-like. Not only were they tame but there were physical changes in some as well. The colour changed, often becoming piebald, showing white spots; ears became floppy; and tails became curly, all dog-like features. This study strengthens the theory that wolves in the wild became dogs rather quickly.[3]

Once the earliest dogs evolved, they began to become specialized. Both the evolving wolf-dogs and the people had something to gain by domestication and humans developed skill at recognizing the characteristics they liked in early dogs. The humans would adopt only the wolves who seemed most friendly or helpful. The people probably thought of the wolf-dog as a pet or closely allied working animal, as we do with horses and guide and police dogs. Some attributes of a pet are more valuable to the human than others. This is how selective breeding would have begun and this led to the many separate breeds of dog we know today. It led to selecting dogs for specific traits, such as strong at swimming or fighting, or good at catching small animal pests. Get a male and a female, both good at rooting out vermin, then get them to mate and they begin producing a race of good, small-game hunter-destroyers. Millennia later, selective breeding led to kennel clubs and the Westminster Kennel Club Dog Show and to the howler of a movie, *Best in Show*.[4] The kennel clubs produce formal definitions of breeds, such as what a dog called a Miniature Schnauzer must be like to be accepted for registry and appearance at dog shows.[5]

🐕 🐕 🐕

The Terrier is not a Retriever. A Retriever goes after the victim of a human's shooting or spearing and carefully brings it back, even if from way out in the water. It will become food or clothing for humans or perhaps a stuffed ornament, but something of value to the shooter. The Terrier either flushes out small creatures – varmints or pests to humans – for the humans to kill or simply finds and kills them himself, on the spot. No one wants the dead body. The French name for these dogs is *chien terrier* (earth dog) which gave us the English name Terrier. My Terrier, recall, walks with his head down toward the ground, sniffing with every step, but he cannot track a tossed object that goes over his head.

Figure 27.   Examples of Crispin's ancestors. On the left, a Miniature Schnauzer puppy. His mother looked like this, only darker in colour. Most Miniature Schnauzers have their ears cropped so they stand up straight. On the right is Kirby, a Wheaten Terrier and former neighbour, a dog like Crispin's paternal grandfather. Kirby is wheat coloured, but in a black and white picture he looks much like Crispin. The Schnauzer image is © iStockphoto.com/Ju-Lee. Kirby comes courtesy of his owner, Max White.

Our particular Terrier is three-fourths Miniature Schnauzer and one-fourth Soft Coated Wheaten Terrier and he shares the history of these breeds. The Schnauzer comes from Germany, developed around the 15th century, the Wheaten comes from Ireland, known only since the 18th century. Both were originally bred to be herders of sheep or cattle as well as hunter-killers of small animals.[6] Both are popular pets. An example of each is shown in the figure above

Dogs and their wolf ancestors, recall, are pack animals. This means they band together in highly social groups, or packs. There are packs of wild dogs still found in some parts of the world, but in most of our North American-Northern European world a dog's pack is more likely to consist of the dog and its human owner's family. Again,

I refer to *The Social Life of Dogs* which includes a fascinating account of packs formed with multiple types of animals, from birds to humans.[7] In the wild, a dog or wolf pack has a leader whom scientists call the *alpha* dog or wolf. This guy is really the boss, not just the chairman. The wolf pack usually consists of a breeding pair and their offspring, possibly more than one generation of them. The alpha is always a male. His principal mate is the alpha female and she may be the only female of the pack allowed to mate but he may mate with other females. The other dogs tend to have a rank, which is understood by all the others.[8] Sometimes, a young dog or wolf will decide to challenge a higher ranking one. This can mean a fight. If the challenger wins, he can take the loser's rank, including the rank as number one. If the alpha is deposed he leaves the pack, likely to become a lone wolf.

There is a gesture called the *play bow* that is used as an invitation to play. The inviting dog puts his forelegs flat on the ground, from toes to elbow, but has his hind legs in the normal, upright position. The head goes down, with a happy expression. This has been interpreted to promise that, in a play fight, no matter who seems to win, the combatants' relative standing in the pack will not be affected by this play fight. In other words, an upset play winner does not unseat the loser. Unseating only happens after real combat or surrender. I once wrote to Desmond Morris, the anthropologist who has made a great study of gestures as a means of communication, asking him if this signal is learned or inbred in all dogs. His reply was inbred, without doubt.[9] It appears to be an important evolutionary development in helping dogs train for adulthood.

The alpha wolf, while leader of the pack, does not necessarily do all the leading. Others may be delegated to lead groups of pack members in a food foray and a low-ranking member may decide to split off and form his own pack. Our human packs, called anything from

Figure 28. This is Bozo, a Yellow Lab, making the traditional play bow. Forelegs from elbow down are on the ground, hind legs almost upright. His mouth is partially open and those familiar with dogs will recognize a non-threatening look on his face. Dogs all seem to know this gesture which invites another dog, and sometimes human, to play. Crispin once made it to a cat. Photo courtesy of Tammy and Daniel Watier.

family to nation state, operate in similar fashion. Rarely is any one person in absolute charge of everything, and a member splitting off to found a new family, tribe or nation is common. In human affairs such a split might lead to war or feuding. It does not appear to be so among the wolves who may form a new pack.

🐾 🐾 🐾

Remember the discussion of why dogs sniff so much, at the ground or fire hydrants, other dogs, or people. The fire hydrant is not a target of choice because dogs have any affinity for fire-fighting apparatus. When dogs mark their turf they prefer vertical surfaces because the smell will carry farther when another dog comes investigating. The mark tells who has been there and can indicate ownership of turf or simply a path to home.

Dogs and wolves have an exceptional sense of smell. A Beagle, for example, may have 50 times the number of odour sensors as humans, a Blood Hound 60 times. That's the number of sensors. In terms of performance, "...the dog has a well-developed and acute sense of smell capable of detecting a variety of substances at concentrations ranging from one thousand to one hundred million times lower than humans can perceive."[10] Imagine the difference in seeing if one person has 1000 times the sharpness of vision as another, or could read from 1000 meters away what an ordinary person could only read from 1 meter. Similarly, a dog can smell, let us say, another dog or food source from what to us is an amazing distance, or detect the odour of a person or dog long gone from the scene.

Dogs can tell a great deal about a person or other dog by smelling that person or dog, especially in the nether regions. They can detect a female dog in heat or a human ovulating. In both species, the key odours come from the areas we consider most private, sometimes leading to embarrassment when a dog sniffs at a human. Some dog owners are even embarrassed when their dog sniffs at another dog's anal area. Dogs can tell much from the odour gathered outside, such as the presence of food, other animals, or other dogs and even which particular dog is at hand. They can detect illegal drugs or explosives in luggage and even illnesses such as cancer in a human.[11]

All this is why dogs spend so much time and energy sniffing. I have seen Crispin much attracted to odors coming from what seems to me a vacant segment of concrete sidewalk.

🐾 🐾 🐾

The main differences between an average Terrier and a Retriever have to do with the latter's innate desire to chase and retrieve and its calm temperament. *Calm* is not a word usually associated with Terriers. Retrievers love the water. Chasing a ball or stick on land or in the water is great fun and good exercise. They were bred because of this desire. In the old days those who were good at it were mated with others who were also good at it, and thereby the races of Retrievers were born. Because they were not built for fighting and don't need to fight to do their appointed jobs, they generally have peaceful demeanors. Some Terriers like to retrieve too, but not Crispin and not other Terriers I have met. He will not chase an object thrown into water that requires him to go in beyond the point where the water goes about to his knees.

If we do toss a ball to Crispin, if it stays on or near the ground, he will chase it. If he gets to it before it stops, he grabs it and sits right down, chewing on his captive. I assume this to be a remnant of his instinct to kill it. If it comes to a halt before he gets to it, he ignores it.

🐕 🐕 🐕

Some people feel that dogs think of themselves as human, probably because they adapt to our way of life so readily. They live in our houses, recognize members of our family and close friends, and as they grow older may show more interest in meeting a new person than a new dog. "Dogs do not think they are people, they think people are dogs." wrote Kathryn Rogow.[12] There is no conclusive evidence for either position, but I have often noticed Crispin when seeing another dog in the distance. He will stop, sometimes sit down, and watch the other dog approach or walk away. He never does this with humans unless it is someone he knows or someone doing something unusual. He will pay attention to cats or squirrels, but not so intently. To me, this clearly means he recognizes the other dog as something different from a person and from other animals.

Crispin may be afraid of a dog he does not know, when he first sights the other and shows his fear by body language or growling. Others do the same to him. I have never seen him do this to a human who does not first do something overt to annoy him. When we go out to an off-leash park, he runs directly to other dogs, rarely to a person, and then only someone he knows.

In the next three chapters we'll talk about what we might call the intellectual and emotional life of dogs – how they communicate, whether they think, how smart they are, and the emotions they experience.

Many people, when thinking about dog or other animal behaviour, have a tendency to project human characteristics onto them. I'm sometimes guilty. I'm ready to swear at times that Crispin is smiling at me. Many scientists simply disregard this as a possibility. Many disagree and some may further feel that any intelligent-appearing response to a human command indicates understanding of our language to some extent. We all love to feel that our dogs love us. This projection of ourselves onto our animals is called *anthropomorphism*, seeing human forms or patterns in non-human creatures or even machines.[13] It can be harmless but also misleading and interfere with our real understanding of the animals we come into contact with. This point will come up again and again in the next three chapters.

Do they really understand the meaning of the commands we give or do they simply develop a conditioned response to certain sounds? Do we humans understand everything we are told to do?

Well, this is mostly news to me. I do remember my mother, but nothing about wolves and breeding, whatever that is. About that business of keeping my head down when walking – I notice that humans tend to keep their heads up and are always looking around at things when walking. I bet I can get more information by sniffing than they can by looking. In fact, I am surprised that humans don't get down on the ground and smell what's been happening. And how much can they tell about another human by shaking hands when they meet instead of sniffing rear ends?

Those retrievers are a bit nuts. Why would anyone go willingly into water? Why spend so much time chasing after a ball? You can't eat it and neither can your pack leader.

As to whether I think of my owners as dogs or a separate breed, well, humans do smell differently, they are very big, they can't run very well, and they never bark. On the other hand, they are members of my pack, and the leader is one of them. There is something different about them but I'm not sure what that makes them. Who cares? We get along.

16 Communication

COMMUNICATION is an absolute essential for a society or organized group of any kind. All mammals that I know of do it, as do birds, even fish. We can talk about a non-communicative person, but that tends to mean a relatively poor communicator. What would it be like to be unable to communicate in any way with other people, yet be aware of what is going on around you? To hear and see, feel touch, but be unable to respond?

Sufferers of the dread disease *amyotrophic lateral sclerosis* (ALS or Lou Gehrig's Disease) gradually lose their ability to move their voluntary muscles.[1] They can see and hear, but at the most advanced stage cannot even blink their eyes. They can be receivers but not transmitters of messages. However, there is some hope that electroencephalography, reading brain waves, can become a means of transmission for these people. The patient would be trained to think about something in particular and the resulting waves might be taken to represent *yes* or a Morse Code dot. A different thought could represent *no* or dash. If the concept were extended, 26 different thoughts could be used to spell out words and maybe someday thinking about a whole word might give a unique and recognizable pattern,[2] hence the ability to communicate directly in words

Students of human language, whether from the view point of linguistics, cognitive science, or literature, tend to be in awe of what we are able to communicate with our human languages and other skills such as dance, mime, drawing, or sculpting. We have learned a great deal about how to communicate with other humans who do not have the same spoken or written language that we do, and a number of humans have become adept at communicating *with,* not just *to,* members of other species. That last point is what this chapter is about, getting beyond SIT or COME or a bark or whine, and reaching the point of meaningful, two-way communication among dogs and other species.

Some of these human to non-human communications have been surprisingly successful, while others have yet to bear fruit. Virginia Morell wrote an article describing a series of successful attempts to teach a variety of animals to communicate with humans. Not surprisingly, the champion seemed to be a Border Collie who had a vocabulary (number of words understood) of more than 300 English words.[3] Less successful, so far, have been attempts to communicate with beings from outside our world, sometimes known as the search for extra-terrestrial intelligence (SETI). The problem there is that we have never knowingly had contact with them, so we do not know if they even exist or, if so, what kind of beings they might be or how best to communicate with them. Marvin Minsky pointed out that we must assume a certain level of our kind of intelligence or knowledge on the part of these beings, or it is hopeless to assume we can communicate over distances of many light years.[4] This brings us back to the lion and the man trying to talk together (on p. 5).

Still another study was from work by Irene Pepperberg with a parrot. The object was to see what the bird's use of language could tell about how his mind worked. The bird learned among other things, to categorize objects as bigger or smaller, same or different, and could count up to six, and carry on conversations.[5]

A friend provided me with a story he claims is true and to which he was an eye witness. It illustrates the vast difference between species even if they can understand each other to some extent, but cannot express their thoughts in the other's language or cannot comprehend why the other cannot speak his language or understand his world.

A rather secular-oriented man was attending a university course in religion. The instructor informed the class that logic alone proved the existence of angels. Borrowing from the venerable "great chain of being" concept,[6] he stated that just as the gap between rocks and humans was filled by intermediate creatures such as dogs, the gap between humans and God, being so great, must necessarily be occupied by intermediate creatures, which we call angels. When the student questioned the logic of this proposition, the instructor glared at him. "Don't you get it?" he asked, with some frustration. "Between rocks and humans there is so great a gap that there must be something in between, such as a dog, correct?" The bemused student could only agree. Pressing the point home, the instructor demanded what this doubter would say if he were a dog and some human denied his place in the hierarchy by claiming he didn't exist. The student thought for a moment and replied, "Woof!" at which point he was ejected from the class. The point of this story is that while the instructor could talk about a dog being asked a theological question, he was outraged by the student responding in the only way a real dog could have responded. I talk to my dog all the time, but he only knows about six words of English. I ask him such questions as "Which way do you want to walk?" I know he doesn't know what I'm saying, but if I'm in a good mood, I'll go in whichever direction he starts walking. What would I do if he turned to me and said, "Woof"?

While I am sure of the authenticity of this story, I was told another involving dog response, this time as action, not words. I cannot vouch for its truth. A family adopted a dog from the shelter, knowing almost nothing about its background except that the former owners were from China, had returned to their home country, and were unable to take the dog with them. From this, the new owners decided the dog must be used to rice. (Reasonable – Crispin loves it and it is normally a major part of a Chinese diet.) So the first meal offered in his new home was a bowl of rice. The dog walked over to it, sniffed, and disdainfully walked away; at least it seemed disdainful to the observer. Then he turned around, walked back to the bowl and peed in it. How much clearer could his message have been?

A third example was provided by Crispin. Periodically, I used to try to teach him to retrieve a thrown ball or some such object. This time we worked inside the house. I threw it, he chased it, but did not return it to me. Instead, he did his usual Terrier thing; sat down and chewed it. I gave him a reward for at least chasing the ball, took it back from him, and tried again. Same result. I tried a third time. This time he ran directly to the steps to our lower storey, went downstairs, and hid under a bed in the guest bedroom. I felt I had received a very clear message. I quit trying.

In the first example, the two communicants, both human, were so far apart in their view and understanding of the world that they could not communicate at such an abstract level. In that example, the instructor asked the student to think how a dog might respond to a question, but was unprepared to accept a message in the only language in which a dog would be able to respond. In the second example it appears that somehow the dog learned to use an action he could take to send a clear message to his people. Or could it be that the people inferred the meaning, which may not have been what was intended? How could we know? The third example was somewhat like the second, in that it did not require that Crispin have previously learned that hiding might have a meaning. Was he simply running away from something he did not like? If so, he may not have been sending a message at all, just escaping. I assumed it was a deliberate message and that suggests rather advanced thinking because it did not directly concern the retrieval issue.

🐕 🐕 🐕

Let's examine what we really mean by words such as communication, language, information, and knowledge. We have to use these words consistently to be able to discuss any of the topics.

Knowledge. This is an old concept. Here is a dictionary entry:

> **a**(1): the fact or condition of knowing something with familiarity gained through experience or association (2): acquaintance with or understanding of a science, art, or technique **b** (1): the fact or condition of being aware of something (2): the range of one's information or understanding <answered to the best of my knowledge>.[7]

Humans had knowledge before they had language. How do I know? The point of language is to be able to transfer knowledge to others. No knowledge, nothing to transfer. Of course, language can also communicate entertainment, but this would have come much later in human development than the ability to tell where the good fishing is or that a predatory animal is coming close. All these words that I want to define have multiple meanings. The important thing, if we want to be understood, is not to insist that only one meaning can be right, but to agree to tell each other which meaning we are using. There have been many academic papers on this subject which you might be interested in reading.[8]

To me, knowledge is, for each of us as individuals, what we know. It is the accumulation and integration of all the messages we have ever received, whether through our genes, our parents' teaching, our own experience, or things we read about. Integration is important. Knowledge is not just a warehouse of received messages. It is what they, together, *mean* to the recipient. It encompasses our world view and it includes a basis for evaluating future messages. It is a safe guess that not everything I think I know is also something you think you know, but many an argument has resulted from not recognizing this. I know my grandchildren are smarter than my brother's grandchildren. Somehow, he does not see it that way. The difference is in the way we have interpreted all the many messages we have received in our respective lives, not just about measuring intelligence, but what we individually treat as important in assessing a child. When raising children or dogs, parents or owners must try to see to it that their charges come to know the "right" things, but we are rarely, if ever, completely successful in this.

Messages. What are these messages I keep talking about? They are sets of symbols sent to another party. "Help!" is a message, with generally understood meaning among English speaking people. "M'aidez!" transliterated from the French into "May Day," is essentially the same message as is S O S (or ••• – – – ••• in Morse Code). This whole book is a message, as is the six o'clock news or a sequence of words the brain gives us when we are required to say something.

When a new message arrives, by whatever means, we must evaluate it in the context of our previous knowledge to see if we can accept its legitimacy. If we accept it, we update our base of knowledge. This is not normally a conscious act. Even if we reject the validity of the message, we may have learned something from it, perhaps only that the sender was unreliable or incomprehensible.

What does a message actually consist of? Symbols, which can be sounds, letters, pictures, odours, tastes or flavors, strokes or punches, strings of DNA. A symbol may have a meaning, such as $, €, or £ or one can have no intrinsic meaning, such as *a*, unless combined with other symbols The letters *a*, *c* and *t* can combine as *cat* or *act*, with two unrelated meanings. Anything can be a symbol, but it is critically important that a symbol or combination mean the same thing to both the sender of a message and the receiver. "Attack at 2" can prove a military disaster if it is not certain the receiver thinks "2" has the same meaning as the sender did. (Is it AM or PM, local time or Greenwich Mean Time?) A simple dog symbol is the position and movement of the tail. Up and waving rapidly signals friendship. Fully upright and slowly moving signals the opposite – both only to a dog or person who knows the code.

Language. This is a set of symbols and rules for their use, mutually understood by a community of people or animals or even machines. The language we humans use is quite complex. In English we use 26 letters plus about 20 more punctuation and common mathematical symbols, and some rules such as how to indent paragraphs, what constitutes proper sentence structure, or that nouns and verbs should agree in number, all this to help us convey meaning. This set of letters (and it really should include the punctuation symbols) is called an alphabet. The basic meaningless alphabetical symbols can combine into words that do have meaning, and the words can be combined into phrases, sentences, etc. to add meaning. It is the marvel of our language how much we can say using only these few basic symbols. We can say things like, "From now on when I say *language*, I mean only the English language." Dogs can't do that. We can embed one language in another without saying we are doing it, as "I was disappointed not to win the prize, but *c'est la vie*." Of course, in print the italics serve as a clue that the words should be treated differently from the rest of the text, in this case as a foreign language, but it is left to the reader to understand in what sense these symbols are to be differently interpreted.

A good dictionary definition of language is, "a systematic means of communicating ideas or feelings by the use of conventionalized signs, sounds, actions, or conditions of associated ideas or feelings."[9] I have one small nit to pick with this definition – the *message* is expressed in a language; *communication* goes beyond language and includes both the process of composing the message and the means of conveying it to a receiver.

Communication.   Humans have many means of communicating. Speaking is probably the most common. There is also writing. There is drawing. There is body language, such as facial expressions and whole body gestures. We can give gifts, kiss each other, hit each other or threaten to do so, or use perfume to attract each other. Not all of us can speak or hear the spoken word or see the written word. Some of us can cope with this by use of Braille and computer software that can transcribe the spoken word into Braille or print into spoken words. Dogs make meaningful sounds, use body language, make gestures, and lick our faces. All these are in effect, symbols in a language that can enable communication. I used to think that each dog's body language was something unique to itself. Visiting in Vancouver one day, a pair of dogs I had never seen before came down the street toward us as we were loading our car. One dog looked exactly like Crispin. His particular mixture of breeds is rare. Yet every gesture the new dog made was exactly what Crispin does. He was immediately friendly with us, and showed it in the same way Crispin does. I can hardly believe he learned this from the same older dog, but if he did not, then is all that behaviour in his genes, possibly learned from a common ancestor?

The physical ways we can receive messages is essentially the same for both dogs and people. We both have the senses of sight, sound, touch, taste, and smell, and no others. Other species, such as migrating birds, can sense magnetic fields and perhaps other phenomena. There are differences in our perceptions with these senses; dogs are much better at smell, we at perceiving colour. There is an enormous literature on this whole subject of various means of communication, some referred to in the Notes.[10]

Both people and dogs sometimes communicate by way of unintentional messages. These are not necessarily errors but messages sent without the conscious intent to do so. This is probably where the expression "Do as I say, not as I do" comes from. The speaker would have done or said something he or she does not want learned by the audience. Hence, listen, don't watch. Children learn a great deal from parents, siblings and friends, without conscious instruction. A common example is a child saying something like, "He eated the cake." Few parents would have taught this form of the verb *eat*. In fact, if the child is, say, two years old, few parents would have engaged in a tutorial on the concept of tense.[11] But the child would have heard many instances of parents adding the *ed* sound to a verb to denote something that already happened and, surely unconsciously, would have sensed that there are words to denote the past, whatever exactly *past* is, and *ed* is the way to show it. This is quite an intellectual accomplishment for a two-year old. Mary Louise and I have seen Crispin learn small things from other dogs who do not seem to be in an instructional mode. The other dog just did something like jump up on a table. Crispin liked what he saw and did it, too.

🐕 🐕 🐕

Now we go to more specifics of how humans and dogs communicate with each other.

Humans to Dogs. Among most people, voice is the principal means of communication to dogs. We also make other sounds than speech, such as screams, whistles, and grunts. Next comes gesture, something humans were certainly doing long before they invented spoken language. This can include pointing, facial expressions such as a single raised eyebrow, threatening gestures, or some form of "come" gesture, such as waving one's finger or whole hand toward oneself, pointing to the ground in front of oneself, or an ASL (American Sign Language) signal. Sheep herders using Border Collies to help control a flock of sheep rely on whistles and hand or arm signals, as well as voice commands, to instruct a dog what to do.

Modern people spend much time with recorded images, such as printing, drawing, or painting, but recording images is no more than about 25,000-45,000 years old (date range of earliest cave drawings).[12] Humans (*Homo sapiens sapiens*) have existed for over 100,000 years and had to have done some form of communication during all intervening time between our cave-drawing ancestors and the huge arsenal of media we have at our disposal today. Watching television is like watching a person and listening to what is said. It's a difference in transmission mode, not so much in what reaches the human eye or ear. These two modes, using sight and hearing, are surely our dominant modes of receiving messages. Feeling, in the literal sense of using our sense of touch, may be next. For blind people, this is one of the dominant modes, but we all learn the hard way not to touch hot stoves. Finally, there are smell and taste. We can't teach calculus or Latin using them, but we can make people feel good or sense danger.

Not all these methods can be used to communicate with dogs who are not much at interpreting recorded messages. They can't read, their colour perception is weak, their odour perception is strong, but they certainly know the difference between a caress and a smack. They have all, but only, the senses humans have, unlike those birds that can sense and navigate by magnetic field or the sun's position.

One day Crispin and I were out walking and stopped for a red light. He sat down, as he should. I looked down at him and noticed he had a large bone in his mouth. I mentioned before his ability to find these things nearly anywhere. I usually silently take the bone away and that's that. This time I did two things: I looked at him with a facial expression that I believe any human over the age of six would recognize as indicating strong disappointment, and I pointed to the ground right in front of him. I did not say anything or make any other gestures. He immediately dropped the bone and made no attempt to pick it up when the light changed and we started walking again. What made him do that? I am reasonably sure I never consciously used that facial expression to him. I have used the pointing gesture. It is commonly part of the training for retrieving; the dog returns with the ball and the trainer points to the ground and says "Give" or "Drop" or some such term. But Crispin never actually returned a ball in any of my attempts at training him. I do use a pointing sign when he has been ignoring a request to come. I say it again, in a sterner voice and, without actually thinking, point to the ground directly in front of myself, where I want him to come. Did he see the drop gesture used by someone else with some other dog? Did he generalize my use of pointing to mean "Do what I just said and do it now"? I just don't know, but I was very impressed at our having reached what seemed a new level of communication between us.

Dogs to Humans. Dogs can communicate to humans or to other dogs in all the ways that people can, except they cannot write or draw. They can make sounds that we can record and play or display to them later, but they have no concept of what a television image means and they usually want more than sight and sound to recognize an image. I have never seen a dog or cat of mine react to a television image of an animal as such. We once had a cat who would sit on top of a TV set and try to catch football players below him on the screen. They may have looked like mice to him. I have seen a dog respond to the sound of barking on TV without looking at the picture, but the response was simply to turn around. The sight of the TV dog meant nothing. I suspect they need odours, anyway more than the sound alone, to make the image seem real.

Dogs speak in their own way. We cannot just say that dogs bark, they bark in different ways to convey different meanings. Their barking repertoire is a language, primitive as it may be. Probably the bark most humans learn about first is the angry or threatening one. This is loud and the basic sound is repeated rapidly. When they want to go out, they use a single woof, usually not too loud. This may be repeated if nothing happens, but there will be at least several seconds between woofs. They also use this low-volume bark when they want attention but are being ignored. There is a happy bark given for example, when the alpha member of the pack returns home and the dog feels it is play time. This may sound like an aggressive bark, but the context is different – no snarling, or display of teeth or tail stiff or slowly wagged. Other sounds are whining, that usually goes with chronic pain or with being tied up or confined; a squeal that comes immediately after being hurt; and growling, a sort of low, continuous bark-like sound used to tell an adversary that an attack might follow if the receiver does not back off.

Dogs may have a large repertoire of gestures – sending a visual message. When begging for food they can look innocent and charming, often sitting because they have been taught that they must do something to earn a treat. Sitting is the most common "something" dog owners require before giving the treat. I believe this is one example of a message they could have learned to use from other dogs as well as from people. When trying to get another dog (or person) to give up a fight before it starts, they can look fierce. When puzzled they have another look and posture, typically standing still and staring at what puzzles them, like a pointer dog, one foreleg lifted. When sleeping, they seem to exhibit total innocence, like a small child. Anthropomorphism may account for this; that is, it is the human observer, not the dog, who provides the sense of innocence, but certainly the dog is not showing any hostile feelings.

Dogs emit a number of odours which another dog can detect and which tell something. Exactly what it tells I do not know but I have often seen Crispin sniff at another dog and seemingly decide on that basis that the other is an enemy or a good friend. He is not alone in this and is as often the victim of a hasty assessment as the perpetrator.

Dogs can use touch to send a message. When seeking petting or attention in general, they may reach out with a forepaw and tap or stroke a person or other dog. They can also use their teeth to great effect to send a different kind of message.

Humans can give gifts that taste good (or, I suppose the opposite as well) to send a message, but I can think of no such instances of dogs sending taste as a message. Cats often bring their owners a choice dead bird and some believe this is given as a gift.

One of Crispin's most charming attributes is the way he makes total strangers smile or even laugh out loud upon seeing him. We walk down the street together and encounter a person coming the other way. Some will just walk by. Many will stop and talk to him or me, clearly delighted with the encounter. Some will just walk by, glancing at Crispin and smiling. He favours women and more women than men reach out to him, but a few men will do the same things. Fewer will stop and express delight at seeing him, but it has happened. I recall one incident when he was less than a year old. We were in line at a bank I had never used before. A male teller came out from behind the counter, approached us and told me this was the cutest dog he had ever seen. Many others will just glance at him, smile, and continue walking. Is this just the accident of his good looks? Or is it something he very subtly conveys, some way of looking at them, some special expression? Whatever it is, it does seem to be communication.

Animals to animals. Animals cannot, of course, write to each other. They are good at gesture, a few of which are described in chapter 19. They also communicate by sound which we cannot present in book form, but here is a picture of two wolves doing what wolves are well known to do, howling. This is not just for fun, it is communication. Wolves separated from their pack might want to tell the others where they are, or ask for a response howl to tell them where the pack is. A human observer might not be able to tell the exact message being sent because the context has much effect on the meaning.

Figure 29. Wolves howling. Once one starts, others join in, but this is not just group singing, it is serious communication, possibly telling where the singers are. Photo © iStockphoto.com/JudiLen.

A cross-species communication example I recently heard about is a fish owned by my friend Giles Hogya. He acquired a tropical fish, a form of tiger fish or *botia dario*, who was ignored while the owners were away for a time. Upon their return they found the water cloudy with algae and the fish appearing somewhat emaciated. Giles fed him (her?) blood worms and recovery was rapid and weight gained. In the tank, as there often is, was a thermometer, affixed to the tank wall by a suction cup. This came loose and one day the fish bumped it, making a noise heard outside the tank. Then Giles came to look and while he was at it, fed the fish. Later the fish bumped the thermometer again, and got the same result. It became a regular, learned behavioural pattern: knock on the tank, get fed. Dogs and cats regularly show such behaviour, but that a fish could learn to communicate effectively to a non-fish is totally new to me.

Figure 30. The fish who "talks" to people by rattling the thermometer in his tank when he wants food. Photo by C. Meadow.

This has been a quick passage through a large subject not yet fully understood but with lots of different points of view. The most important point is to remember that communication requires at least some willingness to try to understand the differences.

Deep stuff, but sounds OK to me. I do hear my owners and other owners using a lot of sounds, I guess you call them words, that mean nothing to me. They seem to think they should.

17 Thinking, Deciding, and Intelligence

A COMMON QUESTION among dog owners and lovers as well as professional researchers, is, "Can dogs think?" The only meaningful response is, "What do you mean by think?"

Many people do not like the notion of dogs thinking because what they themselves mean by it is something rather advanced and complex. It *is* complex, but brains of even lesser animals are wondrous things. These nay sayers see thinking as the very faculty that separates humans from other animals. But that does not tell what it is, only what it might serve to do. To make a decision of almost any kind requires some thought. The very word *decision* implies selecting a choice from among two or more possibilities, even whether or not to stop for an on-coming car or bark at an unfriendly dog. So, if we're going to be thinking about dogs thinking, we have to have at least a minimal definition of what thinking is.

Let us start with decision making. Consider what happens when a dog (anyway Crispin) wants to go outside. He walks to the door. Which door? He knows that the back door leads to our small back yard in which he is free to roam at will. The front door leads to the great outside where he can only go on a leash, but it's also the only portal to the full outside world. He walks to the door of his choice and sits or lies down. Is his decision to go to the door of choice instinctual or learned? I can hardly believe that instinct or genetics taught him where to go if he wants out, and he certainly was not born knowing how to get out of our house. Well, one might think, sitting down is not much of a message. But, picking a door and going to it represents a decision, however trivial, and a decision involves thinking, however minimal. You don't have to be Albert Einstein to decide to go out or to select the appropriate door. But, if Einstein had been unable to open doors in his house, and had some physical problem such that he could not speak, he might have done the very things that Crispin does. He would have thought of some brilliant way to convey his thoughts without words, so replace "Albert Einstein" with "a dog" and maybe you get closer to my meaning.

Now, go one step further. Crispin waits a while at the door and no one comes to do his bidding. What does he do? He barks. In the last chapter, I described his repertoire of barks. Maybe genetics determines which to use in different situations, but he does wait a reasonable time before starting. Another decision.

Does he understand what his bark or his sitting means to us? In other cases evidence exists that dogs *do* learn to expect what some action by them causes in a human member of the pack.[1] Hence, it seems that Crispin did learn what his sitting by the door would mean to us.

Enough. The original question was, "Can he think?" not "What intellectual level of thought does he reach?"

> I seem to be able to make my needs known by barking, sitting, pawing, and things like that. Who needs more? Why all these questions?

At another extreme, hardly anyone would believe that a dog can think to himself such a thought as, "What shall I do tomorrow?" There are two reasons: one, dogs show no sign of understanding the concept of tomorrow, and two, they surely cannot speak to themselves in a human type language. If they have a language at all, it is not English, Russian, Mandarin or anything like them. On the other hand, not all our thinking is done by talking to ourselves; much is subconscious and, if so, does it require use of a language?[2]

> Here you have me. What's "tomorrow"?

Let's take one more example of decision-making. Crispin and someone, normally myself or Mary Louise, but occasionally another person, are out for a walk. At some point he sits down and refuses to move. I usually win these battles; I am more than seven times his weight and I know I can win. Mary Louise wins less often. Usually, his reason for the antic is that his accompanying person wants to go one way and he wants to go another. But it can be that he does not like the weather, rain for example, or does not want to leave his two prime pack-mates behind and go with a relative stranger. Recently, Mary Louise and he were visiting our son, Ben, and Ben decided to take him out. They walked a short distance, then Crispin did his thing – sat down and refused to budge until Ben gave in and returned home. Note: no resistance to returning home. We think he did not want to leave Mary Louise behind in a strange house. Crispin typically sees Ben three or four times a year, less in his own house, knows him, but does not treat him as a member of the inner council of the pack. There may be three reasons for this behaviour, strange direction, bad weather, leaving the closest pack member, and a female at that, behind, but there are still decisions to be made: whether to balk and for how long, each dependent on whom he is with.

🐕 🐕 🐕

What is the relationship of thinking to decision making and what exactly is thinking? One dictionary says, as part of a long entry, "Thinking is the general word meaning to exercise the mental faculties so as to form ideas, arrive at conclusions, etc."[3] Whether in this dictionary or others, definitions of *think* tend to use many equally hard to define words or virtual synonyms. We are essentially left with an intuitive idea of what the word means but we know it encompasses coming up with new ideas and examining alternative possibilities. In terms of decision making, the thinking part is selecting alternatives, determining the costs and potential benefits of each, and selecting the best. The exact processes by which all this cognitive work is done is not something we are fully conscious of. Suffice it to say: decision making requires thinking.

🐕 🐕 🐕

I used to wonder, when Crispin moved from his farm-like home to our apartment house and rode in an elevator, why he was not confused when he entered a room (the elevator car), the door closed then opened again, and he was in a different place. Surely, it was not because he knew what an elevator was. The best explanation I heard is from a noted dog trainer, Cesar Millan, whose answer when asked what we might learn from dogs was, ". . . to live in the moment."[4] Crispin is always here, now. How he got here is of little interest to him. Well, almost here and now. When he sees a dog who resembles one of the ones that bit him six years ago, he shows suspicion, then aggression. Also, remember my describing his memory for houses he has spent time in. There must be some memory of past encounters.

To me, then, the answer to my original question is yes, they think, but in a way vastly different from what we do. Of the traditional *who, what, where, when, why,* and *how* that we are taught in a writing class somewhere between elementary and journalism school, dogs are likely to concentrate on *what,* occasionally on *how.* The why of a situation is least likely to be considered. More and more observers are accepting that dogs can sense time to some extent (i.e., *when*), know what they want or expect to happen next, such as eat or go out (*what*), and recognize places they have been to before (*where*). We will see that even *why* can have its place in a dog's arsenal of cognitive skills, in that he can sometimes tell how another animal will react to something he does, hence, why he does it.

People who have watched a squirrel or raccoon try to reach food when there is a physical barrier in place tend to be convinced that thinking is in progress. My most memorable example was watching a squirrel trying to reach the seed in a bird feeder just a few feet from a young tree that was coated with ice that day. As he walked down the flexible young limbs, his weight would bend the branch so it pointed almost straight down. He could not get enough traction, due to the ice, to stay on it, so he fell off. He tried again and again, each time in some slightly different way. Without the ice or with a sturdier tree he would easily have made it. Finally, he climbed to a higher point on the trunk, but a point much sturdier than the branches, and made a long jump right into dinner. He had solved the problem. Was there no thinking, no decision-making involved? It was not simple selection from among well-defined alternatives. The squirrel had to think what the possibilities were, which were most likely to work, then evaluate why one try failed before trying another.

People who study animal behaviour have not found a generally accepted answer to the question of whether dogs think and if so, how. I am a firm believer that they *do* think. I'm content to leave it that dogs and most animals come equipped with wonderful facilities for perceiving the parts of the world they live in and coping with the situations they normally meet and that they can think enough to make decisions in every-day situations. How their thinking mechanism differs from ours, I cannot say.

> This idea of "think" is a little beyond me. I wonder if you enjoy life as much as I do.

How smart or intelligent are dogs? Of course there are variations and, once again, it depends on what you mean by smart. With dogs, one version is that the most intelligent dog learns the most commands, not just knowing what was asked, but able to execute them properly. Another is problem solving, the ability to decide what to do in situations where a decision is important. Another is ability to track someone from the scent the person leaves or finding his own way home. Jane Packard defined intelligence as "the ability to apply knowledge gained from experience to novel problems."[5] Note that the essence is in *applying* knowledge, not measuring what one knows. All these different aspects, decision making, tracking, and recognizing, are highly useful for a dog, whether living with humans or in the wild. The caliber of decision-making may be the hardest to measure but, at least in my opinion, it may be the most important. Crispin seems good at tracking, if that can include recognizing by scent who is or has been in his house, but was not seen by him. I can't say much for his learning of commands. He knows about six and sometimes gets them confused. He's good at SIT and DOWN (meaning lie down) but sometimes substitutes one for the other. If he does, he always hesitates, indicating he was not clear on what he was supposed to do.

The only test I know of for home measuring of problem solving by dogs came from Elizabeth Marshall Thomas, although there are other tests used in formal studies and dog competitions.[6] Thomas recommended showing the dog to be tested a treat, such as a dog biscuit, then placing it on the floor, covering it with a towel, and waiting to see how long it takes the dog to get the prize. She reported that one of her dogs quickly pulled away the towel and ate the treat. Another pondered for several minutes, then simply gave up and walked away. Crispin solved the problem in 15 seconds. Does that make him brilliant? I don't think so. I've seen him puzzled by how to get from one room of our small house to another, if there is more than one route.

Remember, Stanley Coren estimated that dogs have a mental ability similar to that of a two-year-old child. Of course, both dogs and children vary considerably. In deciding when it is safe to cross a street, I would rather trust most dogs to decide when it is safe to cross a street than a two-year-old child, or even my brilliant three-year-old grandson. But the dog will never grow up to become a Supreme Court justice. Measures such as the popular "IQ (intelligence quotient) test" can predict human performance in some situations, but not all.[7] Its popularity as a factor in determining admission of students to universities does suggest it has done its predictive job there over the years. In 2000 it was reported in the press that Jacques Demers, successful coach of several teams in the National Hockey League, had

never learned to read.[8] If you can't read or read well, you can't score
high on a conventional achievement test (which is to some extent a
measure of knowledge and reading speed as well as of intelligence),
but you can be intelligent. Coaching an athletic team at this level demands a high level of intelligence, quick decision-making, and being
right most of the time. Even his closest associates did not know about
Coach Demers' lack of reading skill. He developed ways to hide that
fact, but he could still get the information he needed to evaluate players and opposing teams' styles of play. The various ruses he used to
cover his illiteracy were, in themselves, an indication of his high intelligence. This affirms the importance of caution in talking about dog
intelligence or, for that matter, any other species' intelligence.

> Humans are funny. You meet a person or dog you like and who
> seems to do interesting things. But right away, instead of just
> enjoying him, you do this funny thing called "measure." Why?

A famous instance of animal intelligence concerned an Austrian
horse named Clever Hans, who in the early twentieth century demonstrated an astounding level of learning.[9] Hans could do arithmetic;
not just count, but even extract square roots, and he could answer
questions in German, using numbers to stand for letters. He was
taught to tap his hoof when asked a question and keep tapping until
he came to the appropriate number. Then he would stop. If asked for
the square root of nine, there would be three taps then a stop. If asked
to spell his name it would begin with eight taps (for H), then a stop.
He would have to be prompted to continue. Then one tap for A, four-
teen for N, and nineteen for S, then stop. He astounded audiences,
including some learned people. His owner and teacher was a highly
reputable man and no one doubted his integrity. Yet, the performance

seemed impossible. To keep the story short, it turned out that as Hans approached the correct stopping number, his owner would unconsciously make a facial expression, showing heightened interest in or anxiety about whether Hans would now stop. Hans learned this meant he was supposed to stop. He performed even if the owner were not in the room, because others who knew the question and answer would make the same facial expressions. What seemed an intellectual feat beyond comprehension was an intellectual feat, but not the one everyone thought it was. No one taught him about the facial expressions. He learned that himself by correlating it with the reward he got for a correct answer. Simple, but it still took some learning ability by Hans, rather like the hockey coach. How many other intellectual feats of animals would have a similar explanation if studied carefully enough? We can't possibly know, but the story is a cautionary one.

Another example of animal thinking that tends not to astound people, possibly because they have been hearing about it all their lives, is the wolf pack attack. Briefly, a pack of wolves attacks a herd of larger animals, such as moose, by tracking them, picking a laggard near the rear, and separating him or her from the herd. They might have a smaller pack hidden in a different place, in case the herd should begin to run away.[10] Once the laggard is separated, they can finish him off without fear of being trampled by the herd. No square roots involved. But, it does require that a plan exist, that younger wolves be trained in how to do it, that the wolf in charge be able to make decisions and communicate them to others in case something goes wrong – again rather like the hockey coach.

Clearly, animals make decisions and decisions require thinking.

You have to be a human to figure this out?

Deception is something many of us do without any malicious intent. Probably a lot of us could do a magic trick that could fool three year olds, but likely not adults. Still, we could be a hit at a tots' party with our fakery. We could play a game of keep-away with a ball, in which two players toss the ball back and forth, always just high enough that the third player cannot reach it. This can get nasty if continued too long, but is often fun for all concerned. Dogs know this game and often play a form of it. One form has the dog bringing a ball or other object to a human, seeming to offer it to him, but pulls away just as the victim reaches for it. Crispin's version of this, when it's time to go home from the off-leash park, is to approach when called, then stop a few feet away, make the play bow, and run away. Repeat n times. This game can be played with another dog; offer some object, then as the other goes for it, pick it up and run. There are stories of much more elaborate scams performed by dogs to get food.

We don't want to get too moralistic about this. It seems very much to be the way dogs are built. They don't have a moral code. What they do have is called a *theory of mind*.[11] This is not a theory of how minds work, but a theory of how a given person or animal will react to a given situation. "What will he do if I come up to him when called to get back on leash, then turn away?" "What will he do if he sees me get on his forbidden sofa?" If the dog is much beyond the puppy stage, he will know the answers to these questions. If he, or a wolf ancestor, is determined to catch a small animal, he knows how that animal is likely to react if the predator shows himself before getting close to the prey and therefore understands the need for stealth. Not the most profound intellectual feat? Maybe not, but how does it stack up against those who insist a dog cannot think at all?

What has this got to do with intelligence? It indicates a possible high order of a certain kind of intelligence – the kind necessary to survive in the wild. Turn this around; a dog who cannot deceive may not be perceived as very bright by the people around him. A dog who does deceive will be judged clever. A fox who acts the same will be considered a menace. A person who deceives regularly might be seen as a criminal, but a poker player who bluffs and wins by a ruse will also be judged clever, but not necessarily crooked.[12]

🐾 🐾 🐾

Many writers have pointed out that *anthropomorphism* can be a barrier to true understanding between humans and animals. What does it mean? My dictionary defines it as "an interpretation of what is not human or personal in terms of human or personal characteristics."[13] When Clever Hans extracted a square root or knew the answer to a question about Austrian politics (so long as it could be answered by tapping his foot), observers might have thought that he was thinking just like humans do; this is an exceptionally brilliant horse. Or, if Crispin shows an unusually affectionate response when we have been separated for several days, it shows he loves me. We'll come to the matter of love in the next chapter, but the point is that jumping immediately to the conclusion that he is expressing human-type affection may not only be wrong but likely to get in the way of true understanding between us. If Hans is not really that clever and Crispin does not really love me that much, it can be and probably was true that Hans was a very clever horse. Crispin may love me in the only way he knows how, by showing the submissive behaviour he would owe to a pack leader in the wild. I'm still free to love him my way. And don't forget, there must surely be as many different meanings of love as there are of intelligence, even in human affairs, but that's for the next chapter.

I'm not sure I really want to know any more about what this is really all about.

18 Emotion – Do Animals Feel and Show It?

IN THE BROADWAY and motion picture musical *Fiddler on the Roof*, Tevye, the hero, musically asks Golde, his wife of 25 years, "Do you love me?"[1] She is astonished by such a question. She ponders and then acknowledges that, after all they have done together, yes, she does love him. What makes the scene poignant is that the question has never before arisen. Before this moment, did either of them know whether they loved the other? Golde's first answer was a recitation of what they had done together and, only after Tevye's insistence, did she agree that she supposed she did love him. If they were just getting to an answer after 25 years, how can I expect to know if my dog of eight years loves me? What is love, to me, and what is it to him? More generally, do dogs feel and show emotions of any kind?

Very loosely, there is the first love of 15 year old high school sweethearts, the love of a parent for a child, of spouses for each other, the love of a patriot for his country, my love of chocolate. The biologist George B. Schaller described love among the snow leopards:

> At times [the two leopards] had ardent reunions, rubbing their cheeks and bodies sinuously and licking each other's face, obviously excited and delighted with the meeting. Witnessing such tenderness, I realized that these leopards merely masked their warm temperament and emotional depth beneath a cold exterior.[2]

Figure 31. While we do not have a picture showing warm affection between leopards, we do have this one of two wolves showing the same thing. Photo © iStockphoto.com/NealITPMcClinon.

And love is just one of many emotions. So, once again we are faced with an important question about the meaning of a word for which we have no clear definition, or we have too many definitions. As a prelude, Winkielman et al. said "... an old line states that there are more emotion definitions than emotion researchers." Then they give their definition:

> Emotion is a state characterized by loosely coordinated changes in the following five components: (1) feeling ... (2) cognition ... (3) action ... (4) expression ... and (5) physiology.[3]

I omitted their definitions of each of these five defining terms, otherwise this would be a very long chapter. What can be seen is that an emotion is more than a feeling; it changes one in terms of thinking and even responding physically.

Here are a few dictionary definitions of one emotion, *love*:

> (1): strong affection for another arising out of kinship or personal ties <maternal love for a child> (2): attraction based on sexual desire: affection and tenderness felt by lovers (3): affection based on admiration, benevolence, or common interests <love for his old schoolmates> an assurance of love <give her my love>[4]

> [a]n intense feeling of deep affection or fondness for a person or thing; great liking.[5]

Note that these definitions are given in terms of words that are near synonyms for love, but are themselves left undefined, especially *affection*, which sounds very much like *love*. So where are we? Could it be that the emotion of love in dogs is a combination of the bonding we have previously described and submission to the leader of the pack? And does the process of bonding create an emotional attachment?

What are all the emotions? A reasonably good list is: contentment, happiness, joy, love, guilt, sorrow, anger, fear, hate, terror. Granted, the difference between happiness and joy or fear and terror may be hard to define, but these terms are in wide general use and are probably generally understood. Also, psychologists make a distinction between an emotion and a mood. An emotion is aroused by something specific; a mood has no specific referent and can be transitory.[6] The tough question is not so much the meaning of the words as how to tell if a being (animal or human) is feeling any one of them and, if so, can express them. Probably for every dog owner who insists that his or her dog expresses one of these emotions, there will be a rigorous scientist who wants proof and who suspects anthropomorphism at work. That brings us back to the question of whether animals experience emotion at all.

🐕 🐕 🐕

Let us look at Crispin and some other animals as they experience, or seem to experience, six moods or emotions: contentment, joy, love, guilt, anger, and fear. We have little choice but to describe behaviour and from that deduce the feelings that led to it.

Contentment. This may not be generally accepted as an emotion. I mean it to apply to a condition in which the dog (or person) is fully relaxed, at ease, at least temporarily not having a care in the world. Dogs and cats feel this because they cannot look much into the future. If nothing is afflicting them now, they don't worry and can be content. All the other emotions to be described tend to involve muscular activity or tensing, changing posture, and intense focus on some one thing or person, dog, etc. So, when we use the verb *emote* we are not normally talking about contentment. But it's a nice feeling. It changes us inside, if not much on the surface. A cat curled up and purring is probably the best example. Dogs can do the same, without the sound effects. It makes you feel good just to look at anyone experiencing this emotion, whether a human baby, a puppy or, a baby rhinoceros.

It is disputed that purring indicates contentment. Cats may also purr when tense, sick, even dying. But exactly why remains a puzzle.[7] Once started, the purring is continuous and does not depend on being petted, although that may be the initial stimulus. Dogs don't make that noise, although Crispin does make little noises that sound like ooh and aah when he is being petted the right way. But he also does what a contented cat does without the sound, just lies down, relaxed, typically with his head on the floor between his paws as in figure 16. He shows no sign of concern with what is going on around him, but if there is activity or noise, he will not do this. He will become alert to the activity. This then is not a major example of emotional behaviour but I picked it for that reason. An emotion can be a feeling of peace and serenity and when expressed it seems obvious how he is feeling.

Joy. Contentment is a happy state, both felt and expressed quietly. Joy in an animal, as in a small child, usually involves vigorous activity. Take Crispin out to the off-leash park on a cool day, take off the leash, and his first reaction is simply to run. He's not going anywhere; he is just feeling great and bounds off, first in one direction, then another. Back in Chapter 9, I described seeing a field full of spring lambs cavorting in this way. Just running and tumbling over each other, no evident purpose except to have fun. Crispin does exactly that, as do most puppies when let loose among a group of other puppies. Some time ago, Mary Louise and I were walking in a wildlife preserve with no other people evident. We came upon a gaggle of geese in a pond. They were cavorting like the lambs, jumping around in the pond, waving their wings, all in seemingly random order. That must have been the origin of the expression "silly as a goose," and that means we were not the first people ever to have witnessed such an exhibition. Finally, I recently saw a young boy, about one year of age, running around his front yard. He was running in circles, screeching, laughing, waving his arms. I guessed it might have been the first time he was let out on his own to be playing outside. Maybe it was the first time he ever had such an outdoor experience with complete freedom to do what he wanted.

All these experiences are pretty much alike. They are expressions of unrestrained joy. They were joyful even to see, let alone to be the one expressing the feeling.

Love. This one is much harder to describe. In spite of all the possible definitions, most of us have experienced it or can imagine what it feels like, but how do we know what two particular lovers are feeling? How do we know what the actions they are showing mean? Can a person, dog, or goose feel love without showing it? The Schaller quote above describes one form of a display of love. Actually, it is fairly common if by love we mean strong affection between living beings and a desire to touch one another. It can, of course, be two people as well as two leopards or wolves. It can be a person and a favored horse or dog, or a cat and a caretaker. (Cats don't quite recognize a pack leader, but they know where the food comes from.) I love a good serving of spaghetti, but I am hardly going to embrace or caress it. A secondary way of showing love among living beings is always, or often, just wanting to be together, not necessarily touching all the time. The problem with this as a proof of having an emotion is that it is hard to tell why the two want to be together – mutual protection, playing games, feeding, or good hunting. This is what Golde and Tevye must have felt.

Elizabeth Marshall Thomas suggested more physical manifestations than merely caressing, in response to the question, "Do dogs have thoughts and feelings?"

Of course they do. If they didn't, there wouldn't be any dogs. That being said, however, a book on dogs must by definition be somewhat anthropomorphic, and reasonably so, since our aversion to the label is misplaced. Using the experience of one species to evaluate the experience of another species has been a useful tool to many of the great wildlife biologists.[8]

She goes on to describe dogs not just mating but establishing a special relationship with one another, enjoying each other's company, not sex alone.

What does Crispin do to display love? Most obvious is his greeting behaviour. It is a great expression of joy, but why? The answer seems to be that he is reunited with his pack or closest human friends who may not be members of the nuclear pack. This, I maintain, comes under the heading of showing love by expressing joy at being with those he loves. Another form of expression lacks the vigor and frequency of this. Crispin is not a lap dog, but sometimes decides he wants to cuddle and hops into a lap. The laps belong to the same few people he vigorously jumps on and what he achieves by hopping into a lap is that feeling of contentment that is important but not so prominently displayed as the greeting.

Crispin has had some affairs with other dogs. It began with Elska. Recall he and she would run to each other when they appeared together in the off-leash park, and ignore all other dogs. They would do the play-wrestling so common among puppies – vigorous physical contact. Then, there came a period when they did not see much of each other and Crispin began to get interested in a female Chihuahua, whose name I have forgotten. Their behaviour was somewhat the same as with Elska, but the Chihuahua never stayed long for any one time in the park. His other close friend, also mentioned earlier, was Jake, the Sheltie. This was a Platonic affair. They did not play much together, but they were always eager to be with each other. Strong male bonding. Love? I know that today heterosexual males who are very good friends, do not tend to use the word love to describe their relationship, although a few hundred years ago, they might have had the same relationship and not shied from the word.

Finally, there is love between species. Everybody I know who has a pet is quite willing to say the word to describe the relationship, at least in the direction human to animal. Even movie cowboys would kiss a horse. The feelings are very strong. Occasionally, there may be love between two animal species. I have see it once between a grown dog and a kitten. I used to believe I would never see it between Crispin and a cat. His Terrier instinct to rid the world of small, non-canine creatures would be bound to get in the way. But recently Mary Louise saw two incidents that suggest otherwise. While walking in the off-leash park they came upon a cat, with a collar and leash attached, sunning itself on a bench. While Crispin's normal reaction would have been to attack, this time he approached slowly, then made the play bow. The cat showed no interest at all and Crispin finally gave up. The next day, the same two were walking on the street when they approached a cat. No play bow this time, but peaceful interest shown by Crispin and sensible withdrawal by the cat. What does the future hold for relations between these two usually hostile enemies? We don't know.

Guilt.   This is often disputed as to its occurrence in animals. I described my former dog, Sam, and his apparent guilt at being caught on the forbidden second floor of our house, and Crispin's apparent learning that an exclusion rule does not mean, "Don't go there," it means "Don't get caught there." A fair number of humans think that way. The appearance of guilt seems obvious; you see a behaviour not shown in other circumstances. The offender slinks away from the person discovering his transgression, tail between legs, not wanting to look at the person, seemingly worried about possible punishment. How different is this from the way a three year old human would act? But, does the concept of guilt actually exist in a dog? Is it not more likely he understands he has transgressed and may be punished? How would we know the difference between guilt and fear of punishment? The manifestation is clearly there but the cause seems unknowable. The conclusion I come to is: case for guilt not proven. It may instead be fear. See more about this in Chapter 19.

Anger. Like joy, anger involves vigorous changes to the body. Blood pressure goes up, muscles tense, hackles stiffen and there are usually facial expressions that make clear the feelings of the person or animal feeling angry. There may be more forceful expressions. For humans this could mean waving the arms about, shouting, shaking a fist, even striking the object of the anger. Our animal friends, except for primates, can't shake a fist or throw things, but they have their ways. A skunk releases an offensive odour; a bird, even without the powerful tools (talons and a strong beak) of an eagle or hawk, "dive bombs," that is squawks loudly and swoops down on its enemy as if to peck it or perhaps pluck out a tail feather. A dog will lower his head, wag his tail very slowly and deliberately, pull his ears back and flatten them, bare his teeth, and growl. All a dog usually wants is to intimidate the target, get the other dog, or occasionally person, to withdraw. This might occur on a walk when we meet a strange dog and one or both takes offense at the presence of the other. The anger intensifies when a dog feels under actual attack or when his food is in danger of being taken away. Then, the growl becomes much louder, perhaps a continuous loud bark, the mouth opens showing the teeth more prominently, and the whole body prepares for combat. While they generally prefer to discourage the other dog, rather than fight, they will fight if necessary. This is true of mentally healthy dogs. The neurotic ones attack and really want to fight, not settling for driving the other guy away. When Crispin was attacked, investigation by animal control showed that both attackers had a history of uncontrolled aggression.

Fear. To me, fear and anger are the emotions I am most certain dogs, cats, horses and the like both experience and show. When Crispin was a young pup, as I described in chapter 6, he could be frightened by loud vehicles such as street cars or subway trains and by large groups of people coming toward him, as would happen downtown at noon or quitting time for office workers. Faced with these horrors, he would cringe, huddle up against a building wall, seem to want to disappear into the solid wall. As he has grown up he is more willing to face the terror, his body tense, his head lowered. He then approaches his possible adversary very slowly, emitting a low pitched growl, tail erect and waving very slowly, teeth might be bared. Crispin cannot move his long, floppy ears. Since he was around six months old he has used this second approach to danger, ready to fight if necessary, however large the adversary. That seems to be another Terrier characteristic. A variation is when he hears the doorbell and barks vigorously, yet calms immediately and becomes friendly when the door is opened by one of us and a human appears. I assume this is momentary fear of the unknown, dispatched by the sight of a friendly figure. Perhaps the barking is purely a reaction to the bell, not to the person ringing it.

Coren gives a brief but well illustrated version of a dog attacking due to fear.[9] Intimidation is a large part of this. One might say that, instead of the standard fight or flight choices in the face of danger, there is a third: intimidation. The difference between fear and aggression can be hard to distinguish, since Crispin's adult reaction to danger is generally to go on the attack, or at least try to intimidate the enemy. Desmond Morris describes a dominant dog's use of intimidation this way:

> If the dominance of the senior dog is challenged, it will perform a threat display in an attempt to subdue the upstart without having to resort to force. Essentially the display does two things: it makes the dominant animal look larger and stronger, and it demonstrates the animal's eager readiness to plunge into the attack, should an attack be necessary. This is usually enough to scare off any rival.[10]

Often, when two dogs get to snarling when approaching each other on-leash, the owners cannot see the cause. It all seems to begin so quickly. One possible reason is given by Coren and by Leaver and Reimchen who both pointed out that dogs give signals with their tails, but a dog without one cannot do so. Dogs without tails or with closely cropped ones, tend to draw more hostile reactions from other dogs than do those with full-length tails. They are simply unable to signal friendly intent.[11] There may be other signals we humans do not catch: slight baring of the teeth, lowering the head on approaching, acting superior to a dog who thinks of himself as superior, too.[12]

🐾 🐾 🐾

To summarize, this has been a review of my own observations and some reading about others' observations. I am aware that some will reject much of what I wrote, but then I reject much of what they write. Jonathan Balcombe recently published a book devoted to "evidence that animals, like humans, enjoy themselves".[13] Another recent book, by Temple Grandin, presents a sense of animal emotions from the view point of a person with autism, giving a greater insight into animal emotions from what most of us have.[14] Clearly, the world is slowly, is coming to agree that animals do have feelings, in the emotional sense of that word. In the next chapter I provide some of the views of scientists in the field and other sharp-eyed observers.

> You do like to use words that don't mean much to me. The way you describe the thing you call contentment sounds like me sometimes. Usually, if I feel that contentment, as you call it, I just go to sleep. Joy, yes, I feel that way lots of times. Love I don't understand. Isn't it the same as joy when you're with the people or dogs you like the most?
>
> Guilt is another word that no one ever taught me, but I recognize some of what you say about it. About this "don't go there" business. If you're home and I get on the couch, you tell me to get off. If you're not home no one tells me to get off. So, I think you mean that I'm not supposed to be on the couch when you are around. Then why are you surprised if I'm on the couch when you come home?
>
> Anger and fear – again I don't know these words, but what you say makes sense. There are dogs that want to fight for no reason and, I've been bit twice by dogs like that. A pup sees lots of things that frighten him. I bet even human pups feel that.
>
> So you say that some humans don't believe that we can be afraid or feel joy? Very strange.

19 How Science Views Emotion – "Are we loved by those whom we love?"[1]

IN THE PREVIOUS chapter I listed ten emotions or moods. Here, I discuss six that Crispin shows. Once again we are faced with important questions about the meaning of words which lack clear definition, or we have too many definitions. To reduce the issue to a single question, it would be, "Do dogs experience and display emotion, or is the behaviour we see as emotion simply a matter of instinct or conditioning?" Sometimes they may purposely hide an emotion, such as the fear following an injury, when an enemy might take advantage of a wounded dog. In this chapter we will mainly hear from scientists, veterinarians, and other sharp observers of nature. I must warn the reader – at the end, the question is not completely put to rest, although I and most authors who live with animals or closely observe them in their natural states, are convinced. Animals *do* feel and show emotion.

🐃 🐃 🐃

How do we tell, or attempt to tell, if an animate being of any kind is experiencing an emotion? Some are obvious: fear, terror, anger or joy. Some are not consciously shown by some people, depending on personality. Machines are used in some cases to detect signs of such emotions as guilt or love.

The polygraph is a machine used to indicate when a human subject is lying or is unusually nervous about some particular question put to him. It works by measuring blood pressure, pulse rate, respiration rate, and skin connectivity or sweatiness.[2] The interpretation is done by a human; the machine simply supplies data about physical changes in the person being interrogated which are assumed to result from a feeling of guilt, fear or excitement. This machine is not in high repute these days, but progress toward measuring a physical reaction to a person's knowing untruth is claimed from new approaches. These are unintended displays of emotion.

If technology could tell a lie from truth, by means of measures of body responses, perhaps it could also determine the amount of joy or fear being experienced. People are also working on such technology.

Recent research work looks at the brain, say through magnetic resonance imaging (MRI) which detects electromagnetic radiation from hydrogen molecules in the brain. By this means it can tell which brain regions are active at any moment. Comparing the patterns of activity with known emotions of a cooperating subject, it becomes possible to compile a list of associations between active brain locations and emotions being felt. When these same patterns are seen in another person, whose emotional state is unknown, it should be possible to tell what emotions that person may be feeling.[3]

Other studies have shown that different emotions in humans cause them to emit different odours. Machines have been used to detect different ones but it does not appear that we are ready for the jump from machine detection of odours to determination of who may be lying or how sincere a declaration of love may be.[4]

The argument, or disagreement, still rages about whether non-human animals can sense and display emotion or have self-awareness, which is the ability to recognize themselves as distinct from others. If you can be aware of yourself, then it is reasonable to assume you can recognize the emotion you are feeling, or at least that you are feeling one. Some recent research is beginning to suggest a much wider variation in non-human perception and display of personality and self-awareness than previously thought possible. I must point out that, in the three examples I am about to describe, the researchers themselves only claim possibilities, not established fact.

Alexander Wilson and Robert McLaughlin did a study of brook charr, a variety of fish, and found differences in behaviour that could be viewed "as personalities or coping styles." There is no indication that these differences were genetic or environmentally caused. The fish studied were young and from a reasonably homogeneous population. Yet, they showed certain distinct personality differences. Tom Spears of the *Ottawa Citizen* commented, "The idea of personalities in animals, obvious in dogs or chimpanzees, but more obscure in fish, is starting to spread across our views of the whole animal kingdom, says Rob McLaughlin . . . who ran the study."[5]

Even further afield, Jim Holt, in the *New York Times*, citing a philosophical concept called *panpsychism*, suggests that since everything in the universe consists of the same kinds of elementary or subatomic particles, even a rock can " . . .'see' the entire universe by means of the gravitational and electromagnetic signals it is continuously receiving." The rock does not do anything with the information it receives, so it has no need to let us know what it "knows."[6]

Michael Pollan described how plants aid in their own propagation by such means as attracting animals to eat their seeds then carry them away and drop them as defecation elsewhere, or by evolving feather-like appendages to the seeds that will enable the wind to carry them away.[7]

A plant can sense light, temperature and the presence of nutrients and respond to an appropriate mix of these elements to grow and produce flowers and fruit or wither and die. Does that mean the plant thinks? Hardly, but it does sense and respond. There is a form of decision-making, primitive as it may be, but more than a rock can do and less than a dog can do. The point here is that responsible people are beginning to stretch our beliefs of what other, lesser species do and feel. A being can think without having the intellectual capacity of a human, and can love or fear without the subtlety of a human.

Can't we just ask the being involved if he, she, or it is feeling a given emotion, or to tell us what feelings are being experienced? The rock, of course, cannot answer. But, I'm sure that every married person has experienced a conversation that goes something like:

Q: Are you mad at me?
A: (Delivered curtly through clenched teeth.) No.

Is the responder angry? Most of us would say yes, but could you prove it in court? Or, how about this conversation:

Q: Isn't this fantastic? Aren't you just overjoyed at the sight of it?
A: Yeah. (Delivered without noticeable emotion.)

Just how happy is the respondent? Has he honestly answered the questions? (I must confess that *he* seemed the right pronoun to use in the previous sentence.) If it is hard to tell about emotion in a human, who is physically capable of answering a question about his or her own emotional state, how can we tell how a dog feels? Let's see what some other writers have said.

☙ ☙ ☙

A question important to deciding whether dogs can feel and express emotion is whether they are aware of themselves as beings. One can hardly know that one is feeling joy or anger if one is not aware of oneself. Anthropologist Elizabeth Marshall Thomas put it this way:

> [Dog consciousness] might seem anthropomorphic simply by definition, since in the past even scientists have been led to believe that only human beings have thoughts or emotions.... [W]hile the question of animal consciousness is a perfectly valid field for scientific exploration, the general assumption that other creatures lack consciousness is astonishing.[8]

Stanley Coren reviewed an experiment done with chimpanzees and another with dogs to determine whether these animals could recognize themselves either by sight (seeing themselves in a mirror image) or smell (recognizing their own urine when specimens were moved from their original placement to places where they were surrounded by samples of other dogs' urine).[9]

Several experiments had been done in which a mirror was placed in a cage containing primates. Often, they seemed to think the image was a member of their own species behind the mirror. In others the animals experimented with making faces and other gestures, recognized that the "other" was doing what they were doing, and thus realized the image was of themselves. But this was not considered conclusive. Finally, one researcher painted red marks on a chimpanzee and watched. The chimp began to touch the areas on his own body on which the red marks had been painted. This was taken as a stronger indication that the animal realized it was himself he was seeing.

Based on data from the dog urine experiment, the researcher concluded, according to Coren, that "dogs do have some aspects of 'body-ness,' the feeling of possessing one's own body and owning the parts of his body, such as 'my paw' or 'my face.' In addition, dogs have a sense of 'mine-ness,' which is the sense of what belongs to him and what belongs to others." In this case the dog recognized his own urine. If in doubt about this feeling, try taking food away from a dog not your own and see if he has a sense of it being *his* food. (Actually, do not do this. It's dangerous.)

I am convinced by these arguments, both because of their logic and because of the people making the arguments.

🐕 🐕 🐕

If we can then proceed on the assumption that dogs have some degree of self-awareness, we can go on to consider whether they have and demonstrate emotions. Charles Darwin in his book *The Expression of the Emotions in Man and Animals* did not bother to debate the question; he described *how* they express their emotions. Here is how he described affection of a dog for its master:

> Dogs have [a striking] way of exhibiting their affection, namely by licking the hands or faces of their masters.... The same principle probably explains why dogs, when feeling affectionate, like rubbing against their masters and being rubbed or patted by them, for from the nursing of their puppies, contact with a beloved object has become firmly associated in their minds with the emotion of love.[10]

The main point here is Darwin's clear conviction that the emotions exist in the dog. Also, in this book Darwin extensively quotes other authors, indicating that belief in animal emotion was widely held.

Patricia McConnell, an animal behaviourist and ethologist, wrote that:

> Emotions are primitive things, centered deep inside a primitive part of the brain. . . . We know that primal emotions like fear and

happiness are critical to survival. After all, emotions allow us to decide between flight or fight. Emotions inform our rational brain about the best course of action."[11]

Here is one more example, this from Nicholas Humphrey, a British theoretical psychologist:

> There are strong evolutionary grounds for believing . . . that the capacity for having feelings has in fact evolved hand in hand with the capacity for expressing them.
>
> The gist of the evolutionary argument is this. The capacity for having feelings (that is, for being consciously aware of them) is an evolutionary adaptation to social life. The capacity for expressing feelings (that is, advertising them) is also an evolutionary adaptation to social life. Hence in any animal in which the former capacity has evolved, the latter capacity is also likely to have evolved, and vice versa.
>
> The idea that the capacity for expressing feelings is connected to social living is perhaps sufficiently uncontroversial for me to take it for granted.[12]

I find this convincing, even though the conclusion is that the author finds the condition convincing, rather than proven by hard evidence. Some things are true without scientific proof.

🐕 🐕 🐕

Now we will review what science says about the same six emotions that were discussed in terms of what Crispin does, in chapter 18.

Contentment. I searched the Web and my books about dogs and found hardly anything from the world of science on contentment. This does not mean that scientists doubt its existence, but more likely they do not consider it an emotion. Advertisers for dog food and food additives frequently mention the term, saying that their products lead to more contented dogs. I can accept this but personally still feel that a sense of relaxation and quiet peace, short of the more energetic feeling of joy is an emotion. Does contentment change bodily responses? It probably slows pulse and respiration rates and lowers blood pressure. But contentment can be long lasting while feeling an emotion typically lasts a relatively short time.

Joy. This is an emotion that almost anyone can recognize in dogs, cats, geese, human babies, or human adults.

The following is what the anthropologist Konrad Lorenz has written. It came after a detailed description of a dog whose expression changed from that when he met another dog to a new one when he met his master. With the other dog he was assertive, with the man ecstatically happy. He then generalizes:

> When this expressive movement [in the dog-to-man encounter] is clearly marked, an invitation to play always follows; here the slightly opened jaws which reveal the tongue, and the tilted angles of the mouth which stretches almost from ear to ear give a still stronger impression of laughing. This 'laughing' is most often seen in dogs playing with an adored master and which become so excited that they soon start panting.[13]

The novelist Thomas Mann described a similar experience with his dog Basham.

> I can produce in him a state of ecstasy, a sort of intoxication with his own identity, so that he begins to whirl round on himself and send up loud exultant barks to heaven. . . . Or we amuse ourselves, I by tapping him on the nose, he by snapping at my hand as though it were a fly. It makes us both laugh, yes Bashan has to laugh too; and as I laugh I marvel at the sight, to me the oldest and most touching thing in the world. It is moving to see how under my teasing his thin animal cheeks and the corners of his mouth will twitch, and over his dark animal mask will pass an expression like a human smile, or at least some ungainly, pathetic semblance of one.[14]

Note that both authors speak of laughter, not joy. But doesn't laughter suggest joy? And Mann brings in the dog's consciousness with his own identity. But, Darwin did use the j-word in this description while saying that there seems *not* to be an evolutionary advantage to being joyful.

> It should be added [to the earlier description of a dog meeting its master unexpectedly] that the animal is at such times in an excited condition from joy; and nerve-force will be generated in excess, which naturally leads to action of some kind. Not one of the above movements, so clearly expressive of affection, are [sic] of the least direct service to the animal.[15]

I think modern psychologists or psychiatrists would disagree with Darwin's conclusion here. Compare the last sentence above with Humphrey's insistence, on page 183, on the evolutionary value of feelings and their expression and social life.

Love. The South Korean firm KTF has recently offered telephone users a service whereby the firm's computers can assess the voice of the person their client is talking with and tell whether the person is truly in love with the client. "[The client] will receive an analysis of the conversation delivered through a text message that breaks down the amount of affection, surprise, concentration and honesty of the other speaker."[16] I am more than somewhat skeptical about this but there it is, an engineering product offered to do the job of interpreting human emotions. Looking at a wider issue, whether a dog who cannot speak our language truly loves us is simply not likely to be resolved by a simple yes-no decision made by a machine. There are matters of trust in the animal, interpretation of signals that the sender cannot define or explain, and that old bug-a-boo, anthropomorphism. Do we feel love because the things our dog does, if done by a human, would indicate love? Or, does the dog do those things because they are what gets him what he wants: food and protection? Reread the quotations from George Schaller and Elizabeth Marshall Thomas in chapter 18.

They clearly believe in love or something like it between animals. Kurt Lorenz wrote:

> The fidelity of a dog is a precious gift demanding no less binding moral responsibilities than the friendship of a human being. The bond with a true dog is as lasting as the ties of this earth can ever be, a fact which should be noted by anyone who desires to acquire a canine friend.[17]

Laura Tangley, editor of *National Wildlife* magazine, wrote, citing the work of two research biologists:[18]

> "Animals at play are symbols of the unfettered joy of life." quoting Marc Bekoff of the University of Colorado-Boulder.[19]
>
> So, too, can be creatures that seem to be in love. The most widespread displays of affection are between parents and offspring. But some researchers also have reported what looks like romantic love. Bernd Würsig, a Texas A&M University biologist, was studying right whales off the coast of Argentina when he saw a female choose just one of many suitors pursuing her (in contrast to "normal" behaviour marked by promiscuity). After mating, the two whales lingered side-by-side, stroking each other with their flippers, then rolled together in what looked like an embrace. Finally the cetaceans departed, yet remained touching as they swam away slowly, diving and surfacing in unison.[20]

The Würsig observation and interpretation is surely an oceanic version of Schaller's observation. We can only conclude that scientists more and more believe in such emotions as love in animals.

Guilt. Stephen Budiansky, a noted science writer and owner of several breeds of animals, is somewhat agnostic on this point. He says

> [A]ll dogs are house-trained by being taught to associate their act of defecation–or the presence of dog poop on the floor and ourselves on the scene–with punishment. So the condition the dog has to learn in order to display what we take for guilt is actually quite simple: dog poop in the house plus a person equals trouble. As social animals, dogs as a matter of course and quite instinctively display a variety of behaviours of submission.... So is it guilt, or is it merely ap-

peasement of aggression that the dog has been conditioned to anticipate under these circumstances?[21]

Uh oh. This one hits hard. I believe dogs *do* show emotion. I did not ever punish Crispin for pooping on the floor, because he did not do it, except once when seriously ill. It is possible that his mother punished him. Also, I have pointed out my belief that both Crispin and my former dog Sam seemed to accept exclusion rules as meaning don't get caught. Why not get caught? There would be consequences. Note that Budiansky gave as conditions for feeling guilty, both poop on the floor *and* a person in the house. So, I cannot refute him. Fear of possible punishment may be Crispin's version of guilt. In fact, might it not be the same for humans?

Lorenz described similar behaviour when he brought a new dog into his home, to share space with an older dog who had been with him for some time. The two dogs began to fight. Lorenz separated them but, in the process, was bitten, apparently accidentally, by his old dog, Bully (his name not his description).

> Bully … incurred the severest shock to the nervous system that a dog can ever receive: he broke down completely and although I did not admonish him and indeed stroked and coaxed him, he lay on the carpet as though paralysed, a little bundle of unhappiness, unable to get up…. His bad conscience affected me the more in that my own was anything but clear towards him."[22]

Using Budisansky's theory, Bully might have been expecting a severe punishment for attacking the alpha member of his pack.

Anger. Dogs show anger when frightened or threatened. An example is any dog when any other dog, or sometimes person, takes away his food or threatens to do so. Another is a small dog, such as Crispin, being approached by a much larger dog bearing some resemblance to one that once bit him. Barking is a sign of anger, but is not conclusive proof of it. An Israeli company called Bio-Sense Technologies has technology that it claims can tell whether a dog is genuinely responding to a threat or "just routinely woofing." It is used primarily in security work to alert help if a guard dog is barking to express a real threat.[23] Below is a quotation from Darwin on the anatomy of the subject.

> When a dog approaches a strange dog or man in a savage or hostile frame of mind he walks upright and very stiffly; his head is slightly raised, or not much lowered; the tail is held erect, and quite rigid; the hairs bristle, especially along the neck and back, the pricked ears are directed forwards, and the eyes have a fixed stare…. As he prepares to spring with a savage growl on his enemy, the canine teeth are uncovered, and the ears are pressed close backwards on the head.
> Hardly any expressive movement is so general as the involuntary erection of the hairs, feathers and other dermal appendages; for it is common throughout three of the great vertebrate classes. These appendages are erected under the excitement of anger or terror; more especially when these emotions are combined, or quickly succeed each other. The action serves to make the animal appear larger and more frightful to its enemies or rivals, and is generally accompanied by savage sounds.[24]

A hostile dog, from Darwin's book is shown in figure 31. Note that he said the dog would draw his ears back and flat as he got closer to his enemy. This is to lessen the chance of the other biting him on the ear or grabbing it in his teeth. That would occur later in the encounter than what this picture shows. Crispin's hair is medium long, typically five centimeters in length, which he cannot raise as does a short haired dog or cat, and he has floppy ears which he cannot move forward or flatten in back. But, he can get very angry. Also, he *always* lowers his head when approaching a dog of whom he is suspicious. Compare the illustration from Darwin with that of an angry, not

Figure 31. A dog "with hostile intentions" as perceived by Darwin's illustrator, identified only as Mr. Riviere. The tail is up and stiff, the hackles are raised, the ears forward, but the look on his face doesn't seem terribly hostile. From *The Expression of the Emotions.*[25]

Figure 32. An angry dog, ready to fight if necessary. There seems little doubt what is on his mind. Photo © iStockphoto.com/carebya.

merely hostile, dog in figure 32. Another dog should have no difficulty in reading this one's message, while the face alone in Darwin's illustration could be misread, at least by humans.

Fear. Veterinarian Debra Horvitz describes fear as

> . . . the interaction of physiologic, emotional, and behavioral re-
> sponses and is not necessarily a maladaptive behavior. When an
> animal encounters something unfamiliar, potentially dangerous, or
> simply not understood, a fearful reaction can prepare it to deal with
> the problem.
> A dog may show any or all of the following: lowered body and
> head, pupillary dilation and/or piloerection [otherwise known as
> raising the hackles – CTM], ears pulled back tight to the head, bark-
> ing, growling, snarling, lunging, snapping, biting.[26]

Fear sometimes causes the dog to withdraw and sometimes to decide to attack. It is hard to imagine a higher animal – dog, cat, horse,
chimpanzee or other primate – who cannot sense fear. Here, again, we
see the evolutionary benefit of displaying an emotion. Perhaps of all
the emotions this should be the easiest for us humans to recognize in
other species because their reactions are so much like our own.

🐕 🐕 🐕

I have mentioned several mechanical systems used to detect some
emotion in a person being interrogated, a person expressing love on
the telephone, or a guard dog who may or may not have been excited
by an intruder. John Seabrook wrote an interesting article about computer systems used to converse with humans. These are called *interac-
tive voice response* systems (IVR) and are increasingly popular with
large companies.[27] Whether they work well or not, they are much less
expensive than hiring humans. Getting a machine to understand human speech is difficult enough. Add to this the necessity to detect the
emotion of the speaker or to understand a complex question and it all

leaves me often wondering why companies do not realize the harm a poor IVR system may do to their customer loyalty or even legal liability if the guard dog attacks the wrong person. But, in limited cases, they show promise of accomplishing their mission. One example Seabrook described is found in Groningen, Netherlands. Microphones were placed in public areas where many pubs are found. If the computer connected with these mikes detects the sounds of aggression from people in the crowd, police are dispatched. A city official was quoted as saying, "Groningen is the safest city in Holland. We don't have enough aggression to train the system properly." This, of course, could mean either that the system does not work well but no one knows it, or that Holland is a very safe country.

🐕 🐕 🐕

So far in this and the previous chapter I have concentrated on what Crispin or his canine peers might be feeling, and various authors' opinions on the subject. We also need to consider what I feel toward him, what he feels toward me, what I want from him and what he wants from Mary Louise and me.

Let's start with what he wants from us. The obvious ones are food, shelter and security. But, he wants more than that. He clearly wants affection demonstrated by a willingness to play with him, pet him, be with him, and let him have his way sometimes on a walk when he wants to explore and we might rather get on with the walk. In return, his greatest gift is loyalty. This seems to be inborn in dogs and wolves but is nonetheless appreciated. In addition, one of Crispin's more endearing acts is to jump unbidden into a lap, get petted of course, but also "pet" by licking the hands of the person holding him and possibly just curling up and going to sleep. Crispin does not lick faces. When he comes into my lap I know we have bonded, that he doesn't merely want things from us, he also wants to give something. We are talking here about not just anyone but one of his pack mates or a special friend of long standing.

What do I want from him? I want what I just described as the things he gives. I want him to like being with me, to want to show his liking the only ways he knows how.

How do I feel about him? I love him, not as I love my wife, children, and grandchildren, but he is a member of my family. Love for us humans is quite complex and likely to be different between any pair of people; different between parent and child, between a parent and his or her own parent, or between siblings or spouses. I owe Crispin loyalty and he owes me loyalty. I owe him affection and he owes me affection and the two of us get and give a great deal of both.

🐕 🐕 🐕

I've written a lot about human sensing of dogs' emotions, such as noticing the various ways dogs express them. Let us consider the other side of this, how dogs sense our emotions or those of other animals. Formal science has little to say on the matter. This seems to come under the heading of understanding complex phenomena, hence often to be dismissed as impossible. As usual, those who live with dogs disagree, at least to some extent. That dogs can sense certain emotions in other dogs is a necessity for survival. I have seen my own Crispin show intense hostility when he felt I was showing too much affection to my daughter's dog. I mentioned a friend telling me that her dog resented affection between her and her husband. These emotions may be relatively easy to detect, but they do tend to show that such capability can exist, at least at some level. Evolution, then, requires that this capability have developed or the dogs might not have developed fully.

There are many cases reported of dogs sensing illness or sadness in a human. There has been some technological study on detection and interpretation of odours, somewhat like the use of technology to detect lying in a human. A Rice University study[28] started with the knowledge that all human bodies produce certain odours which are likely to change as emotions change. Suppose we could detect all the odours emitted by humans, classify them according to what gender, age, or race they came from and the state of the human they are identified with, then see what physiological changes occur with certain emotions, such as fear or tension. Then, following the logic used with the MRI studies, we might detect the emotions of a human automatically. If a machine can do it, why not a dog? Is all this a bit too far out? Maybe. But it does suggest a path of research that might someday bring practical results and, if subtle odour differences do tell the story, why cannot dogs with their fabulous odour detection apparatus be able to make these decisions?

🐕 🐕 🐕

Did I finally answer the question at the top of this chapter? No matter how much I read and think about it, the answer keeps coming up the same – it depends on what you mean by love, not only what you or I mean, but also what the dog means.

I'm afraid this means nothing to me except that, once again, I wonder why you humans spend all this time thinking about what has no meaning. Love, loyalty, call it what you want. It's what dogs do and people talk about.

🐾

V Recognition

In which our hero is advanced to a royal position in his adopted city and receives the tributes due him.

20 The Number One Dog in Victoria

I WAS SITTING at my desk, one day, working on this book, when the telephone rang. The conversation was as follows:

CTM: Hello

Voice: Is this Charles Meadow?

CTM: (*Hesitantly*) Yes.

Voice: This is Victoria Animal Control Services.

CTM: (*Not speaking or interrupting, but dying a little. What could Crispin have done?*)

Voice: (*Continuing*) Do you have a dog named Crispin?

CTM: (*Now terrified*) Yes

Voice: He has been chosen Dog of the Year (2007) in Victoria. Congratulations.

CTM: How wonderful! (*that I survived the phone call.*)

I can't remember the rest in detail. I was still focused on the law suit that sounded sure to be raised at the end of this call. As my mind returned, I assumed that Crispin had won a contest based on his good looks and intelligence, as well as those same characteristics of his owner.

Wrong. It was a random draw from the records of all dogs who were licensed in the city for that year.

The caller was Ian Fraser, head of Victoria Animal Control Services, whom I had met twice before, in connection with Crispin's two attacks by larger dogs.

Fraser asked if he and the Acting Mayor could come to our house to present the award. We were delighted. I couldn't help wondering how Ian had managed to convince the Acting Mayor of a busy city to take the time off for this occasion.

Do it they did. We were presented with a replacement dog tag – Number 1 for 2007 – as well as a gift certificate from a dog food and supply company and a nice picture of Victoria's Acting Mayor Charlyne Thornton-Joe, Crispin, and me.

Figure 34. The big prize. Photo by C. Meadow.

It may not sound like much, but we milked it for all it was worth with family and friends most of whom clearly drew pleasure by their association with a celebrity of this magnitude. No one else in the family was ever declared Man or Woman of the Year. Crispin took it all in stride, as befits a true leading dog, and he has enjoyed his new bed, procured with the gift certificate. This chapter was written in 2008, when we had all returned to our common old selves.

Crispin, in his eight years with us, has been a delight as well as a cause of trouble. What it all comes down to is: Do we love him or not? Does he love us or not? We know we love him. We know that in his own way he loves us but that his way of loving is different from ours. So? He's always Number One dog to us.

Those visitors were nice enough, but they didn't bring any food.

Figure 35. Acting Victoria Mayor Charlyne Thornton-Joe presents Crispin with the new Number 1 license and a gift certificate. Photo by Ian Fraser, Victoria Animal Control Services.

Notes

Citations here are in abbreviated form, usually serving as a link to the complete citation in the Bibliography section following. A citation to a portion of a book, usually shows only the author's last name, an abbreviated title of the book, and the pages referred to. A citation of an article in a journal, newspaper or book gives the author's last name followed by the name of the article. A referral to a web site varies because the web sites themselves vary so much. If an author is identified, we start there, then the title. If the publisher of the material is known, that follows the title. When either an article or web site has no identified author, it is alphabetized by the title, with articles, *A*, *the*, etc. ignored. Watch out, both here and in the Index, that many URLs necessarily are split over more than one line and the unseen RETURN character is *not* part of the address. Some of what appears here are comments by the author.

Chapter 1
   [1] Wittgenstein, 1998, 223.
   [2] Levy, "Navigating with a Built-in Compass."
        Wikelski, 'Sixth sense."

Chapter 2
   [1] Jung, "The Pueblo Indians" in *The Spell of New Mexico*, 41.
   [2] There are many variations of this. Some say it was part of a letter, others a speech. Some say it never happened. It is supposedly Chief Seattle's response to a proposal by President Franklin Pierce that the area under the Chief come under control of the United States. There are other versions. Even the spelling of the name of the Chief's tribe is subject to variation, another form being Duwamish. However mysterious, it represents a point of view generally attributed to native Americans. The version given here is from "Chief Seattle's

Thoughts," which see.
More information can be found at:"Chief Seattle" and "Chief Seattle's Famous Speech."

Chapter 3
[1] Whether there actually was a St. Crispin is somewhat in doubt.
See Delaney, *Pocket Dictionary of Saints*, 132.
[2] Brown, *Mr Dog*.

Chapter 4
[1] Siegal & Margolis, *I Just Got a Puppy*.
[2] Prado, *My Guy Barbaro*. Specific quotes: "Racing fans. . ." 2; "first commandment" 148; "forming bond..." 70; "Then Barbaro came along..." 149.

Chapter 5
[1] "Care of Mother Dogs and Puppies."
[2] Morris, D., *Dogwatching*, 24-26.
[3] Darwin, *The Expression of the Emotions*, 28
Budiansky, *The Truth About Dogs*, 59
Morris, D., *Dogwatching*, 27-28.

Chapter 9
[1] Jefferson, "Letter to Abigail Adams."
[2] Coren, *How Dogs Think*, xii.

Chapter 10
[1] Mech and Boitani, *Wolves*, 123
[2] Budiansky, *The Truth About Dogs*, 165.
"The Arctic Wolf."
[3] Monks of New Skete, *How to Be Your Dog's Best Friend*, 78-81.
[4] Darwin, *The Expression of the Emotions*, 32.

Chapter 11
[1] "Dog-having-a-blast-in-the-snow" web site.
[2] "Spear Grass: What You Should Know."
"Plants Profile: Hordeum marinum."
[3] Abrantes, *Dog Language*, 168-71.
Shaw, "An Overview of Gait."

Chapter 15
[1] Busch, *The Wolf Almanac*, 1

Clutton-Brock, "Origins of the Dog."

Grzimek's Animal Encyclopedia.

Nowak, "Dogs, Wolves, ..."

Serpell, *The Domestic Dog*, 2

[2] Morey. "Early Evolution of the Domestic Dog."

[3] Trut, Lyudmila N. "Early Canid Domestication."

Morey, "Early Evolution . . . "

[4] *Best in show.*

[5] "Miniature Schnauzer Breed Standard."

[6] Fogle, "Terriers," 252-89."

"Miniature Schnauzer History."

[7] Thomas, *The Social Life of Dogs*, 153-176. Describes an example of dogs and other animals forming packs while living with a human family. The author is an anthropologist who has written many books about people and about animals. A beautiful book.

Packard, "Wolf Behaviour: Reproductive, Social and Intelligent."

[8] "Understanding Pack Behavior."

[9] Personal communication, Desmond Morris to C.T. Meadow.

[10] Serpell, *The Domestic Dog,* 107.

More information is available in Coren, *How Dogs Think*, 50-80.

[11] Coren, *How Dogs Think*, 79-80.

[12] Rogow. "10 tips for successful dog ownership." Ms Rogow writes here as a lawyer, warning against us thinking of dogs as people and pointing out that they do not think like people.

[13] Coren, *How Dogs Think*, 289.

Chapter 16

[1] "What Is ALS?"

Merck Manual, 330-332.

[2] Winters, "Communicating by Brain Waves."

[3] Morell, "Inside Animal Minds."

[4] Minsky, "Communication with Alien Intelligence."

[5] Pepperberg, "Talking with Alex" and *The Alex Studies.*

[6] Facchini, F. "Evolution, Emergence and Transcendence of Man."

"The Great Chain of Being."

[7] *Webster's Seventh New Collegiate Dictionary*

[8] Meadow and Yuan, "Measuring the Impact of Information: Defining the Concepts." This paper contains a lengthy bibliography of other writings concerned with definitions of words like *information, knowledge*, etc. as used in different fields of study.

[9] *Webster's Seventh New Collegiate Dictionary*

[10] Yule, *The Study of Language*.
   Altman, *The Ascent of Babel*.
   Chomsky, *On Nature and Language*
   Darwin, *The Expression of the Emotions*.
   Gurney, *The Language of Animals*.
   Morris, D. *Bodytalk*
   Morris, D. et al, *Gestures*
   Pinker, *The Language Instinct*.
   Savage-Rumbaugh, *Ape Language*.
   Sebeok, *Signs*.
   Ullman, *Ancient Writing*.
[11] Pinker, *The Language Instinct*, 21.
[12] Marshack, *The Art and Symbols of Ice Age Man*.

Chapter 17
   [1] Dodman, "Can Dogs Sense Our Emotions?"
   [2] Pinker, *Words and Rules*.
   [3] *Webster's New World Dictionary, 1960*.
   [4] Newman, "The Dog Whisperer."
   [5] Packard, "Learning and Intelligence" in "Wolf Behaviour: Reproduc-
        tive, Social, and Intelligent."
   [6] Thomas, *The Social Life of Dogs*, 31-32.
   [7] "Concepts of Intelligence."
   [8] "Former NHL Coach . . . ."
   [9] Budiansky, *If a Lion . . .*, xxx-xxxv.
   [10] "Wolfbehavior."
        "Hunting Behavior."
   [11] Budiansky, *If a Lion . . .*, 157-58.
        Coren, *How Dogs Think*, 308-11.
   [12] Coren, *How Dogs Think*, 312-17.
   [13] *Webster's Seventh New Collegiate Dictionary*.

Chapter 18
   [1] *Fiddler on the Roof*.
   [2] Schaller, *Golden Shadows*, 196.
   [3] Winkielman et al., "Emotion, Behaviour, and Conscious Experience."
   [4] *Merriam-Webster Online Dictionary*.
   [5] *Oxford Canadian Dictionary*.
   [6] Morris, W., "More on the Mood-Emotion Distinction."
   [7] Lyons, "Why Do Cats Purr?"
   [8] Thomas, *The Hidden Life of Dogs*, xvii
   [9] Coren, *How to Speak Dog*, 251.

[10] Morris, D., *Dogwatching*, 43
[11] Leaver & Reimchen, "Behavioural Responses."
[12] Coren, *How to Speak Dog*, 115-133
[13] Balcombe, *Pleasurable Kingdom.*
[14] Grandin and Johnson, *Animals in Translation.*

Chapter 19
[1] Alexis, Andre. "Andre Alexis Remembers the Past." This quotation
is from a book review by Mr. Alexis.
[2] Archer, *The Lie Detectors.*
"The History and Basic Facts of Polygraph"
"The History and Evolution of Lie Detection"
[3] "Human Brain Operates Differently In Deception And Honesty."
"MRI: The Ultimate Lie Detector?"
[4] Chen and Haviland, "Human Olfactory Communication of
Emotion."
[5] Spears, "Study Finds Animals Have Personality."
Wilson and McLaughlin, "Behavioural Syndromes In Brook
Charr...."
[6] Holt, "Mind of a Rock."
"Panpsychism."
[7] Pollan, *The Botany of Desire.*
[8] Thomas, *The Hidden Life of Dogs,* ix-x.
[9] Coren, *How Dogs Think*, 305-308.
[10] Darwin, *The Expression of the Emotions*, 65-66
[11] McConnell, "A Glass Half Full."
[12] Humphrey, *"Consciousness Regained,"* 43.
[13] Lorenz, *Man Meets Dog,* 61
[14] Mann, *Stories of a Lifetime*, 97.
[15] Darwin, *The Expression of the Emotions*, 32.
[16] "How Deep Is Your Love?"
[17] Lorenz, *Man Meets Dog,* 139
[18] Tangley, "Natural Passions."
[19] Bekoff, "Beastly Passions."
[20] Würsig, B. "Leviathan Love." in *The Smile of a Dolphin: Remarkable Accounts of Animal Emotions*, M. Bekoff ed. New York: Discovery
Books/Random House. New York, 2000.
[21] Budiansky, *If a Lion Could Talk*, 25-26.
[22] Lorenz, *Man Meets Dog*, 86-87.
[23] Heller, "From Yap to Growl."
[24] Darwin, *The Expression of the Emotions*, 53.
[25] Horvitz, "Fearful Dogs."

[26] Seabrook, "Hello, HAL"

[27] Darwin, *The Expression of the Emotions*, 31.

[28] Chen and Haviland, "Human Olfactory Communication."

Bibliography

Abrantes, Roger. *Dog Language*. Naperville IL: Wakan Tanka Publishers, 1997.

Alexis, Andre. "Andre Alexis Remembers the Past." Question raised in a book review in Toronto *Globe and Mail*, 29 Jan. 2008, D13.

Alder, Ken.*The Lie Detectors : The History of an American Obsession*. New York : Free Press, 2007.

ALS Association. "What is ALS?" Web site: http://www.alsa.org/als/what.cfm

Altman, Gerry T.M. *The Ascent of Babel*. Oxford and New York: Oxford University Press, 1997.

"The Arctic Wolf" Web site: www.cosmosmith.com/arctic_wolves.html

Balacombe, Jonathan. *Pleasurable Kingdom-Animals and the Nature of Feeling Good*, London and New York: Macmillan, 2006.

Bekoff, Marc. "Beastly Passions." Web site, animalliberty.com/animalliberty/articles/marc-bekoff/marc-14.html

————. "Deep Ethology" Available on web as: http://cogprints.org/161/0/199710001.html

Best in Show. Motion picture. Produced by Gordon Mark and Karen Murphy, Directed by Christopher Guest, Distributed by Castle Rock Entertainment., 2000.

Brown, Margaret Wise. *Mr. Dog*, Little Golden Books, New York: Simon and Schuster, 1952.

————. *Goodnight Moon*. Most recently published by HarperFestival, in New York, probably available in many other editions.

Budiansky, Stephen. *If a Lion Could Talk*. London: Weidenfeld & Nicoloson, 1998.

————. *The Truth about Dogs*. New York: Viking, 2000.

Busch, Robert A. *The Wolf Almanac*. Markham ON: Fitzhenry & Whiteside, 1998.

"Care of Mother Dogs and Puppies," in *Veterinary Practice STAFF*, Vol. 5, No. 5 September/October 1993. Also in Web site: www.hilltopanimalhospital.com/whelping2.htm.

Chen, D. & Haviland-Jones, J. "Human Olfactory Communication of Emotion." *Perceptual and Motor Skills*, 91, 2000, 771-781.

"Chief Seattle" in "Rediscovering North American Vision," *In Context,* Summer 1983.

"Chief Seattle's Famous Speech." in web site
www.chiefseattle.com/history/chiefseattle/speech.htm.

"Chief Seattle's Thoughts." Web site
www.kyphilom.com/www/seattle.html.

Chomsky, Noam. *On Nature and Language.* Cambridge: Cambridge University Press, 2002.

Clutton-Brock, Juliet. "Origins of the Dog: Domestication and Early History," in *The Domestic Dog,* ed, James Serpell. Cambridge: Cambridge University Press, 1995.

"Concepts of Intelligence" In"Stalking the Wild Taboo," which see.

Coren, Stanley. *How to Speak Dog.* New York: Fireside, 2000.

———. *How Dogs Think.* New York: Free Press, 2004.

Darwin, Charles. *The Expression of the Emotions in Man and Animals.* My copy was published in 2005 by Digireads,.com Publishing, Stilwell KS. The original publisher, in 1872, was John Murray, London UK.

Delaney, John J. *Dictionary of Saints,* Abridged ed., Garden City NY: Image Books, 1983.

Dodman, Nicholas. "Can Dogs Sense Our Emotions?" Web site:
www.petplace.com/article-printer-friendly-.aaspx?id=4329

Dog-having-a-blast-in-the-snow. Web site:
www.Maniacworld.com/Dog-having-a-blast-in-the-snow html

Facchini, F. "Evolution, Emergence and Transcendence of Man." Web site:
www.academiavita.org/template.jsp?sez=Pubblicazioni&pag=testo/cult vita/facchini/facchini&lang=english

Fiddler on the Roof. Stage play. First produced by Fred Coe and Harold Price, Directed by Jerome Robbins. Opened in New York in 1964.

Fogle, Bruce. "Terriers" in *The New Encyclopedia of the Dog.* Willowdale ON: Firefly Books Ltd., 2000.

"Former NHL Coach Jacques Demers Admits He's Illiterate." Web site
www.cbc.ca/sports/story/2005/11/03/demers051103.html

"The Great Chain of Being." Web site:
academic.brooklyn.cuny.edu/english/melani/cs6/ren.html.

Grandin, Temple and Catherine Johnson, *Animals in Translation: Using the Mysteries of Autism to Decode Animal Behavior.* Orlando: Harcourt, 2006.

Grzimek's Animal Encyclopedia. 2nd ed, Vol 14, Mammals III. Devra G. Kleiman, Valerius Geist, and Melissa C. McDade, eds. Detroit: Gale, 2003.

Heller, Corinne. "From Yap to Growl, Israeli Device Dogs Intruders." Web site www.reuters.com/articlePrint?articleld-USL 19773582 20070103

Holt, Jim. "Mind of a Rock." Web site
nytimes.com/2007/11/18/magazine/18wwln-lede-t.html?_r=2&oref=sl ogin&ref=magazine&pagewanted=print&oref=slogin.

Horvitz, Debra. "Fearful Dogs." Web site:
  www.hilltopanimalhospital.com/fearful%20dogs.htm
"How Deep Is Your Love?" Web site:
  www.reuters.com/articlePrint? artcleid=USSEO26301720080214.
"Human Brain Operates Differently In Deception And Honesty." Web site
  www.sciencedaily.com/releases/2001/11/011112073302.htm.
Humphrey, Nicholas. *Consciousness Regained: Chapters in the Development of
  Mind.* Oxford and New York: Oxford University Press, 1983.
"Hunting Behavior." In Mech and Boitani, 119-122. Also available at web site:
  http://books.google.ca/books?id=_mXHuSSbiGgC&pg=PA119&lpg=PA
  119&dq=%22hunting+behavior%22+wolves&source=bl&ots=cNc00prVk
  c&sig=0qRUDVS1H4DVh33se3WClAoOaZ8&hl=en&sa=X&oi=book_res
  ult&resnum=3&ct=result
Jefferson, Thomas. "Letter to Abigail Adams," 1787, in *The Writings of Thomas
  Jefferson,* Paul Leicester Ford, ed., New York: G. P. Putnam's Sons, 1892-
  99, 370 and on the Web at
  www.let.rug.nl/usa/P/tj3/writings/brf/jefl55.htm.
Jung, C.G. "The Pueblo Indians," in Tony Hillerman, ed., *The Spell of New
  Mexico.* Albuquerque: University of New Mexico Press, 1976, 37-43.
Leaver, S.D.A. and T.E. Reimchen. Behavioural "Responses of *Canis familiaris*
  to different tail lengths of a remotely-controlled life-size dog replica."
  Behaviour, 145, 2 Nov. 2007, 377-390. See abstract at
  uvic.ca/~reimlab/S.Leaver%20-%20Reimchen%20Lab%20page/
  S_Leaver.html.
Levy, Sharon. Navigating with a Built-In Compass, in: *National Wildlife Maga-
  zine,* 37(6), Oct/Nov 1999. Also at Web site:
  www.nwf.org/nationalwildlife/printerFriendly.cfm?issueID=26&articleI
  D=682.
Lorenz, Konrad Z., *Man Meets Dog.* London, Methuen & Co., 1954.
Lyons, Leslie A. "Why Do Cats Purr?" *Scientific American Online.* Web site:
  www.sciam.com/article.cfm?id=why-do-cats-purr
Mann, Thomas. *Stories of a Lifetime,* vol. 2. London: Secker & Warburg, 1961.
Marshack, Alexander. "The Art and Symbols of Ice Age Man." David
  Crowley & Paul Heyer eds. New York: Addison Wesley Longman, Inc.
  1999, 5-14.
McConnell. Patricia B. "A Glass Half Full," web site
  http://thebark.securesites.com/ezine/commentary_columns/Patricia_
  McConnell_Dog_Behavior_39.html
Meadow, Charles T. and Weijing Yuan. "Measuring the Impact of Informa-
  tion: Defining the Concepts." *Information Processing and Management,*
  33(6) 1997, 697-714.

Mech, L. Davis and Luigi Boitani, eds. *Wolves: Behaviour, Ecology and Conservation.* Chicago: University of Chicago Press, 2003.

Merk Manual of Medical Information. Home Edition, R. Berkow, M. Beers, and A. Fletcher eds. Whitehouse NJ: Merk Research Laboratories, 1997.

Merriam-Webster Online Dictionary. Web site: www.merrian-webster.com/dictionary.

"Miniature Schnauzer History" Web site: www.breederretriever.com/dog-breed-history/176/miniature-schnauzer.php.

"Miniature Schnauzer Breed Standards." Web site: www.akc.org/breeds/miniature_schnauzer/index.cfm. For information about other breeds and rules, see www.akc.org/.

Minsky, M. "Communication with Alien Intelligence" In *Extraterrestrials: Science and Alien Intelligence.* E. Regis, ed. Cambridge: Cambridge University Press, 1985.

Monks of New Skete, *How to Be Your Dog's Best Friend.* Boston: Little, Brown and Co., 1991.

Morell, Virginia. "Inside Animal Minds," *National Geographic,* 213(3), 2008, 36-61.

Morey, Darcy F. "Early Evolution of the Domestic Dog," *American Scientist,* 82(4) Jul-Aug 1984, 336-347.

Morris, Desmond. *Dogwatching.* London: J. Cape, 1986.

———. *Gestures: Their Origins and Distribution.* London: J. Cape, 1979.

Morris, Desmond et al *Bodytalk.* London: J. Cape, 1994.

Morris, William N. "More on the Mood-Emotion Distinction." Web site: www.cogsci.ecs.soton.ac.uk/cgi/psyc/newpsy?3.07

Newman, Cathy. "The Dog Whisperer," *National Geographic,* v 210, no. 6, Dec. 2006, 33-37.

Nowak, Ronald M. "Dogs, wolves, coyotes, jackals and foxes," in *Walker's Mammals of the World,* Baltimore: Johns Hopkins University Press, 1995.

The Oxford Canadian Dictionary. Oxford University Press Canada, Don Mills ON: 1998.

Packard, Jane M."Learning and Intelligence" in "Wolf Behaviour: Reproductive, Social, and Intelligent," in Mech and Boitani, *Wolves,* 63-65.

"Panpsychism." Web site of *Stanford Encyclopedia of Philosophy,* plato.stanford.edu/entries/panpsychism/.

Pepperberg, Irene. *The Alex Studies: Cognitive and Communication Abilities of Grey Parrots."* Cambridge: Harvard University Press, 2000.

———. "Talking with Alex: Logic and Speech in Grey Parrots." *Scientific American Exclusive Online Issue.* Web site: randsco.com/_img/blog/0710/talking_with_alex.pdf

Pinker, Stephen. *The Language Instinct.* New York: William Morrow and Co., 1994.

―――.*Words and Rules: the Ingredients of Language.*New York: Basic Books, 1999.

"Plants Profile: Hordeum marinum." Web site: plants.usda.gov/java/ profile? symbol=HOMAG

Pollan, M. *The Botany of Desire.* New York: Random House, 2001.,

Prado, Edgar and John Eisenberg. *My Guy Barbaro: A Jockey's Journey Through Love, Triumph, and Heartbreak with America's Favorite Horse.* New York: HarperCollins, 2008.

Rogow, Kathryn V. "10 tips for successful dog ownership." Web site

Schaller, George. *Golden Shadows, Flying Hooves.* New York: Alfred A. Knopf, 1973.

Seabrook, John. "Hello, HAL." *The New Yorker, 23 June 2008, 38-43.*

Sebeok, Thomas A. *An Introduction to Semiotics.* Toronto: University of Toronto Press, 1994.

Serpell, James. *The Domestic Dog, its Evolution, behaviour, and interactions with people.* Cambridge: Cambridge University Press, 1995.

Shaw, Linda, "An overview of gait" Web site
www.shawlein.com/The_Standard/08_Overview of_Gait/Overview of Gait.html

Siegal, Mordecai and Matthew Margolis. *I Just Got a Puppy. What Do I Do?* A Fireside Book. New York: Simon & Shuster, 1992.

Spears, "Study Finds Animals Have Personality." Web site:
www.canada.com/topics/technology/science/story.html?id=a7d908ee-8379-4de5 -8be4-bb64ef0f741e.

"Stalking the Wild Taboo" Web site
www.lrainc.com/swtaboo/taboos/apa_01.html. Board of Scientific Affairs, American Psychological Association, 1995.

Talbot, Margaret. "Birdbrain," *The New Yorker,*,12 May 2008, 64-75.

Tangley, Laura. "Natural Passions" in *International Wildlife* Sept/Oct 2001. Also in web site:
segate.sunset.se/cgi-bin/wa?A2=ind0110&L=ethology&P=68.

Thomas, Elizabeth Marshall. *The Social Life of Dogs: The Grace of Canine Company.* New York: Simon & Shuster, 2000.

―――, *The Hidden Life of Dogs. New York: Pocket Books, 1993.*

Trut, Lyudmila N., "Early canid domestication: the farm fox experiment," *American Scientist,* 87(2), March-April, 199.)

Ullman, B.L. *"Ancient Writing and its Influences"*Toronto: University of Toronto Press, 1989.1980 © Medieval Academy of America

"Understanding pack behaviour" Web site of Izat Italian Greyhounds, 2004, at www.italian-greyhounds.net/packbehave.htm

Webster's New World Dictionary of the Engliosh Language. Cleveland: World, 1960.

Webster's Seventh New Collegiate Dictionary. Springfield MA: G & C Merriam Co., 1963.

"What Is ALS?" Web site: www.alsont.ca/about-als/.

Winkielman, Piotr, Kent C., Berridge and Julia L. Wilbarger, "Emotion, behaviour, and conscious experience," In Lisa Feldman Barrett et al, *Emotion And Consciousness*, New York, The Guilford Press, 2005.

Winters, Jeffrey. "Communicating by Brain Waves." Web site: www.psychologytoday.com/articles/pto-20030724-000002.html

Wikelski, Martin. "Sixth sense: Study shows how migrating birds navigate." Web site: www.princeton.edu/pr/news/04/q2/0428-wikelski.htm.

Wilson, Alexander D.M. and Robert L. McLaughlin, "Behavioural Syndromes in Brook Charr, *Salvelinus fontinalis*: Prey-Search in the Field Corresponds with Space in Novel Laboratory Settings." in *Animal Behaviour*, 74, 689-698, 2000.

Wittgenstein, Ludwig. *Philosophical Investigations*, 2nd ed. Trans. G.E.M. Anscombe. Oxford and Malden MA: Blackwell Publishers, 1998.

"Wolfbehaviour." Web site www.freewebs.com/alphawolfsabrina/huntingbehaviour.htm.

Yule, George. *The Study of Language*. Cambridge: Cambridge University Press, 1985.

Index

The Index is arranged in the normal way except that there are so many subheadings under Crispin and Dogs in General that each of these has a sub-index for it alone, as these two terms occur in alphabetic order within the whole index. The subindexes are in bold italics. Also the initial C in any entry means Crispin.

CRISPIN

END DOGS IN GENERAL